# The Yellow Story Book

## Enid Blyton

*Text illustrations by Jenny Chapple*

Dragon

*She tapped the beak with her wand*

## The Untidy Gnome

The Untidy Gnome was in a great state of excitement because he was going out to Mr. Dumpy's birthday party. Mr. Dumpy always gave wonderful parties, with ice-cream and lemonade, pink and yellow jellies and the biggest balloons you ever saw.

The Untidy Gnome had a new suit for the party. He felt very grand in it, because it was bright blue, rather tight, and was trimmed with hundreds of little red buttons.

"I mustn't eat *too* much in case the buttons go pop," thought the Untidy Gnome, looking down at the buttons. "They would go 'ping, ping, ping', all over the place, and make people laugh. I hope I remember not to eat too much. I always seem to forget, once I begin eating anything nice."

He looked out of the window to see if his friend Dame Bustle-Round was coming. She had promised to call for him. Ah, yes – there she was, looking very fine indeed in a new red skirt and a bright yellow shawl. She had on a wonderful bonnet with what looked like a whole garden of flowers around it! She bustled up to the door and the Untidy Gnome opened it.

"Untidy, have you got your umbrella?" panted Dame Bustle-Round. "It's *just* beginning to rain, and I can't possibly have my new hat spoilt. Look at all the lovely flowers on it."

The Untidy Gnome looked. He had never seen such a flowery bonnet in his life. He nodded his head. "It

5

would certainly be a pity to spoil that bonnet," he said. "And I don't want my suit to get wet either, Dame Bustle-Round. You see, it's rather tight, and if it shrinks a bit, I'm sure all the buttons would pop off, ping, ping, ping!"

"Well, get your umbrella quickly then," said Dame Bustle-Round. "I am late. Where is your umbrella, Untidy?"

"It should be in the umbrella-stand," said Untidy. "The only thing is – I'm not very good at putting things back in their proper places, you know. Still, I *hope* it's there."

They both looked in the umbrella-stand, which was a big tall pot. It had a walking-stick in it, and something else. Dame Bustle-Round looked in astonishment.

"*Potatoes!*" she said. "Untidy, why do you keep potatoes in your umbrella-stand?"

"Well, so that's where my potatoes are!" said Untidy, surprised. "Of course – I remember now, the potato-box was full of something or other, so I put them there, and then I forgot about them."

"Well, for goodness' sake, put them in the right place," said Dame Bustle-Round. "I wondered what the funny smell was in your hall. I'll get the potato-box and we'll empty them in. Where's the potato-box?"

"Under the kitchen sink," said Untidy. So they went to get it. It was quite full of something. Dame Bustle-Round pulled out the box to examine it.

"Untidy! This potato-box is crammed full of stockings!" she said. "Whatever made you put them here? Where do you usually keep them?"

"Well, dear me, I wondered where they were," said Untidy, joyfully. "I haven't been able to find a pair of

6

stockings for days! Yes – I remember now – my darling cat, Pippy, had some dear little kittens in my wardrobe, where I keep my stockings, just at the bottom you know. So, to give her more room I took out the stockings and put them here."

"Now, Untidy, this won't do," said Dame Bustle-Round, sternly. "I like Pippy, but she is not to be allowed to live in your wardrobe. Bring your stockings, and we will go upstairs and turn her out. She and her kittens can go down into her basket. It's quite big enough."

They went upstairs with the stockings. The wardrobe door was open, and in the bottom, surrounded by shoes, was Pippy, the cat, with four dear little kittens. She purred loudly when she saw Untidy and Dame Bustle-Round.

"Naughty little cat!" said Dame Bustle-Round. "Why don't you take your kittens to your basket? Shoo now, shoo! I'll carry your kittens and Untidy shall carry you."

Dame Bustle-Round picked up the kittens, and put Pippy into Untidy's arms. She threw back the stockings into the wardrobe, shut the door and went firmly down the stairs to the kitchen. She looked round for Pippy's basket.

It was in a corner – but it was full of something black. Dame Bustle-Round stared in horror.

"Coal! Coal in the cat's basket! Untidy, have you gone mad this week? Why put coal in the cat's basket? No wonder the poor creature went to your wardrobe!"

"Well, the coal-scuttle was full of chicken-food," said Untidy, taking a look at it. "You see, Jinky said he would give me some chicken-food if I took round something to put it in, so as the coal-scuttle was the first thing that came to hand I took that. So I had to put the coal somewhere else, and the cat's basket was handy."

"Coal in the cat's basket, chicken-food in the scuttle, cats in the wardrobe, stockings in the potato-box – really, it's like a bad dream!" said Dame Bustle-Round. "Untidy, take the chicken-food out to the bin, please; and then put the coal in the scuttle. Then I can perhaps put these kittens into their basket."

Untidy carried the scuttle of chicken-food to the bin in the yard just outside. He opened the lid, and was just about to empty in the food when he gave a loud cry of delight.

"Ooooh! So this is where all my new books got to! Dame Bustle-Round, all my new books are here. Isn't that lovely?"

"Well, I shouldn't call new books in the chicken-food bin lovely," said Dame Bustle-Round. "For goodness' sake, Untidy, empty that coal-scuttle, and bring it back and put the coal into it. I'm getting tired of carrying these kittens."

Untidy emptied the food into the bin, all on top of the new books, hurried back into the kitchen, and put the coal into the scuttle. Then Dame Bustle-Round popped the four kittens into their dirty basket, and Pippy the cat got in on top of them, settling down in delight.

"Where did you put the books?" said Dame Bustle-Round, looking about. "Surely, Untidy, you didn't leave them in the bin?"

"Well, you sounded in such a hurry," said Untidy. "I'll just go and get them." He rushed out to the bin and put his arms into the food. He groped about for the books and brought them out. He banged them together, because they were covered with food, and the dust flew all over his new suit.

"What a sight you look," said Dame Bustle-Round. "For goodness' sake, put the books on to the book-shelf, and let's go to the party before you get any dirtier."

"But we haven't found the umbrella yet," said Untidy, in despair. "We've found a whole lot of things, but we really haven't found the umbrella."

"Untidy, do put those books on to the shelf," said Dame Bustle-Round, getting cross. "Are you thinking of taking them to the party with you?"

"No, but there doesn't seem to be room on the book-shelf," said Untidy, looking at it.

Dame Bustle-Round looked too. The bookshelf was piled with red roof-tiles! She gazed at them in astonishment.

"What are you going to do with all those roof-tiles?" she said at last.

"Well, you see," said Untidy, "there's a tile off my roof, and the rain comes into the bedroom and makes a puddle. So I bought some tiles, and this morning I went up on the roof to put the tile on."

"And did you put it on?" asked Dame Bustle-Round.

"Well, it began raining," said Untidy. "I did take my umbrella up there to hold over me, but I couldn't seem to hold it up and put the tile on, too, so I came down again."

"You had your umbrella up on the roof this morning, then!" said Dame Bustle-Round. "Did you bring it down with you?"

"Now I come to think of it, I don't believe I did," said Untidy, trying to remember. "No, I can't have

9

brought it down, because I remember that I had my arms full of tiles and I couldn't hold it. So I shut it and came down without it."

"Well, you must have left it on the roof then," said Dame Bustle-Round, annoyed. "Thank goodness we know where it is. I might have thought that would be where you kept your umbrella – up on the roof – or at the bottom of the well, or in the piano!"

"I'll go and see if I've left it there," said Untidy. So he went out and looked up at the roof. But he couldn't see the umbrella there. His ladder was still standing, leaning against the roof, so he went up it. He stood on the roof, holding on to the chimney, wondering where in the world he could have put that tiresome umbrella.

Then Dame Bustle-Round suddenly heard him give a shout. "Here it is! I've got it! Hurrah!" and down the ladder came Untidy, waving a very sooty umbrella about.

"Where was it?" asked Dame Bustle-Round.

"In the chimney," said Untidy. "You see, I shut it and popped it into the chimney, hanging the handle on the rim of the chimney-pot so that it wouldn't go down the chimney."

"Well, next time I want your umbrella, I'll look in the chimney-pot," said Dame Bustle-Round, in disgust.

"What do you keep in your teapot? White mice, I suppose. I think you are the silliest person I ever knew. Oh, Untidy, *don't* open that sooty umbrella all over me!"

Untidy felt offended. He stalked off beside Dame Bustle-Round, holding the umbrella over himself and not over her. They didn't say a word till they arrived at Mr. Dumpy's.

10

*He stood on the roof*

"I hope you are not wet," said Untidy, in a cold and polite voice.

"Not at all," said Dame Bustle-Round, also very politely. "It hasn't been raining all the way here, and the sun has been shining brightly. But, of course, I couldn't expect you to notice all that. After all, if you keep umbrellas in chimney-pots, you probably only use them when the sun is shining."

Poor Untidy felt very small and silly. He stood his umbrella carefully in the stand, and walked in to the party. And, alas, he quite forgot about not eating too much, so very soon there was a ping, ping, ping noise, and little red buttons flying all over the place. Mr. Dumpy gathered them up and gave them all to Untidy when he went home.

"Now, mind you put them somewhere safe till Dame Bustle-Round can come and sew them on for you," he said. "Be sure to put them in your button-box."

"Button-box!" said Dame Bustle-Round. "*He* won't put them in a button-box! He'll put them inside the clock – or into the pepper-pot – or scatter them around for the chickens to eat. *He* won't put them into his button-box!"

*I* don't think he will either, do you? He's just too silly for words!

## The Two Runaways

For about the first time in his life Robin shut a door quietly. Nobody must hear him going out, nobody must see him rushing down the path to the back gate – he was running away!

"I'm fed up with everything," he kept saying to himself. "Fed up with doing the kitchen fire, fed up with tearing off to school and back again to do more jobs, fed up with being the eldest of a horrible family."

He shut the back gate behind him. Now he was in the lane. He would go to the end of it, walk up the hill and catch the bus to the next town. Then he would go down to the docks – and if he couldn't get on a ship somehow or other his name wasn't Robin Linton.

"Nearly fifteen – and always having to do this, that and the other for mother, never a minute's peace. Keeping the twins in order, little beasts, reading to Mary – well, she can't help having to lie on her back so much, I suppose – and rushing round trying to find out what mischief Jack's got into. Getting in the wood, helping to wash up, not having any money of my own. And then mother says, 'Robin, you are the man of the family since Dad's gone,' and thinks that's good enough to make me lead the life I do. Well, I'm going to have a life of my own now."

He thought about it as he went up the hill to get the bus, shifting his bag of belongings from one shoulder to another. He was big for his age. He could surely get a job on a ship – and then he would be off to another

13

country, he'd see the world, he'd be a man. And he would never, never go back home again to see all the people who had kept him so hard at work. They were just so many chains that tied him down.

There was no bus waiting at the top of the hill. "Blow!" said Robin. "It's gone. Now I'll have to walk. Or perhaps I can hitch-hike – it would be fine to get a lift in a car."

He thumbed this car and that, but nobody stopped for him. Then at last a smart little car came by, with a middle-aged man driving it. He stopped when he saw Robin. "Want a lift, son? Hop in. Where are you going?"

The man was burly and his face was very brown. Robin thought he was an American by his speech, but he turned out to be a Canadian. He was soon telling Robin all about his "wunnerful" country.

"Now, son," he said at last, after they had gone about ten miles. "Where exactly do you want me to put you down? Are you off on a visit somewhere?"

Robin went red and turned his face away. He was afraid of saying that he was running away in case the man took him to the police-station or something like that.

"I just want to get down somewhere near the docks," he mumbled. The burly man looked at him sharply. He saw that the boy had on what must be his best suit. He noticed the bursting bag of belongings. What was the boy up to? Was he running away?

"You're not running away, by any chance, are you?" he said. When Robin said nothing, he swung his car into a side-road, pulled up, and stopped.

He turned and looked at Robin. Nice-looking boy – very nice – bit sulky perhaps, and needed a hair-cut.

*Robin was running away*

Good wide-set eyes, strong and healthy-looking. Had he done something wrong? Was he running away in case the police were after him?

"You know," said the man unexpectedly. "I was a frightful little coward too, once. *I* ran away, just like you! I got fed up with things at home, and off I went. Ran away, instead of facing up to them."

Robin was startled. "*Did* you?" he said. "But – from all you've told me, it was a very good thing for you. You went all over the world – you settled down in Canada, and had a fine ranch. You made a lot of money."

"Yes. I gained a whole lot of things," said the Canadian. "And I lost a whole lot too. For one thing, I lost my family when I ran away. I was hard, I wouldn't write, not even to my poor old mother. Now she's dead. How'd you like it if you heard your mother was dead, all of a sudden, and it was too late just to tell her you were sorry, and you *had* loved her, even though it didn't seem like it. I didn't even send her a present."

Robin thought suddenly of his own mother. She was often tired and cross – but she was kind to him and proud of him. And she had a lovely smile when ·he came home from school. No – he wouldn't like it at all if he heard she was dead. He was going to run away all right – but he would send her a letter quite often.

"Then I had a sister," said the Canadian, lighting a pipe. "Prettiest thing you ever saw – bright blue eyes and curly brown hair, and a smile that was like the sun coming out. Well, I lost her too. She got married, I heard, and went away. I could never find out where. And I had a young brother – I detested him then because I had to look after him. But he was a merry, cheeky fellow, and how I'd like to have him now."

"Haven't you anyone now then?" said Robin.

16

"Not a soul," said the man. "My wife died, and I've no children. I'm rich and I've got friends. But they're not family. To think I threw away my mother and my sister and my brother, and ran away from my stupid little difficulties! Well, my boy, I tell you, I was a coward, just like you – but if you've a mother and sisters and brothers, don't throw them overboard. Stick by them whatever you do!"

"Well, but I'm *not* running away," said Robin, surprising himself very much. "My mother needs me because my father's dead. And I'm the eldest of the lot. I'm not runnng away, so don't think it."

"Pleased to hear it, son," said the Canadian, and shook Robin solemnly by the hand. "And all I can say is – if I had a kid brother like you, I'd be proud of him. Come on – we'll go back the way we came and I'll drop you at your home."

And, without another word, he drove all the way back. When they got to the bus stop on the hill, Robin showed him the way to go to his home. They stopped at the little front door.

Robin's mother ran into the garden. "Robin! Where have you been? I found your clothes had gone – oh, I was so afraid you'd run away, like your Uncle Tom did, years ago."

The big Canadian was just putting in his clutch to drive off when he heard Robin's mother calling all this out. He stopped suddenly and leaned out of the car. He stared so hard at Robin's mother that she drew back, offended.

Then a strange thing happened. The Canadian got out of the car, walked through the gate like a man in a dream, and took Robin's mother by the hands.

"Bess!" he said. "It's little sister Bess! *Don't* say your

17

name isn't Bess. You've still got the same blue eyes. Smile at me – let's see that again."

And Robin's mother smiled. Her blue eyes were suddenly bright with tears. "It isn't *you*, Tom – not after all these many, many years is it?" she said. "Oh, Tom – our mother's dead – but I'm here, and our brother isn't far away. And you've got nephews and nieces – here's Robin, one of them."

"Yes. I've met him," said her brother. "But he's a better boy than I ever was, Bess. He's not a coward – *he'll* never run away and lose you all. Don't you think it! That's right, isn't it, Robin?"

Robin nodded. He couldn't speak. Things were happening so fast, he could hardly make head or tail of them. But he knew one thing all right – he was never going to run away from ANYTHING again.

And then he came to life, and became the noisy, eager, high-spirited boy he always was. He rushed into the back garden, yelling.

"Hey, Mary – Jack, twins, where are you? Come here and see what *I've* got. A big surprise."

The twins flung themselves on him. "Oh, Robin – we thought you'd run away. You made Mother cry."

"Pooh – run away indeed! As if I'd ever do a silly thing like *that*," said Robin. "Aren't I the man of the family?"

18

## The Enchanted Book

This is a queer story. It is about John, a boy who lived forty years ago in London. John is grown up now, of course, and he doesn't know if it was all a dream, or if it really happened. You must decide for yourself when you read the story.

John was eight years old. He was just an ordinary boy, going to school every day, working, playing, eating, and going to bed at night, just as you do.

He was naughty sometimes, just as you are. He was kind sometimes, just as you are. When he was naughty his mother and teachers scolded him. When he was kind they loved him. Sometimes they said: "You *must* be honest. You *must* be patient. You *must* be unselfish."

But they didn't tell him exactly *why* he must. He thought about it a little, and then he said to himself: "I don't see that it matters very much if I tell a little fib now and again. No one will know. And if I buy sweets and eat them all myself, why shouldn't I? No one will know. And what does it really matter that I took Harry's rubber the other day and didn't give it back? He didn't know I took it. As long as nobody knows, I can't see that it matters."

And then one day something happened to him that showed him the real reason why all those things did matter.

At that time John was sort of half-and-half. That is, he sometimes told the truth, and he sometimes didn't. He was sometimes kind and sometimes unkind. He was sometimes quite honest, and sometimes not. A lot of children are like that. John could be very mean and spiteful and rough – but he could also be very generous and unselfish and gentle. He was just about half-and-half. Half-good, and half-bad.

Now one day, when he was still a half-and-half, he went shopping by himself. He went down an old, old, street in London, peering into shops that sold old, old things. They were dusty, and they looked sad and for-gotten. There were curious mirrors with dragons carved round the frames. There were old china ornaments – spotted dogs and funny cats, and some shepherdesses with sheep. There were old chairs, some of them so big that John half wondered if they had belonged to giant men.

He saw a dear little work-basket that had once be-longed to an old lady many years past. On the lid were two letters made of mother-of-pearl. They shone pret-tily. The letters were M.L. John stared at them, and a thought came into his head.

"M.L.," he said to himself. "Mummy's name is Mary Lomond. What fun if I bought that basket for her birthday! I'll ask how much it is."

He went into the shop. The funniest old man came out of the dark part of the shop – rather like an old spider coming out of its web, John thought.

"How much is this basket, please?" asked John.

"Ten shillings," said the old man.

John stood and thought. He had almost ten shillings at home – but he had meant to buy himself a knife with three shillings of it. He badly wanted a knife. All the boys in his class had a knife except John. If he spent all his money on the basket, he wouldn't be able to have

20

the knife. So, after thinking for a while, John shook his head.

"I've only about five shillings," he said. This wasn't true, but he didn't want to explain to the man that he almost had enough but wanted to spend some on himself. The old man nodded.

"Look around and see if there's anything else," he said. He hobbled off and left John in the untidy, musty, dusty old shop. The boy began to look round. He looked at a set of old games. He tried all the drawers in a funny old desk. He looked at some of the old books on a shelf.

And it was there he found what he always afterwards called the Enchanted Book. It was an enormous book, and the covers shone queerly, almost as if they were on fire. When he was looking at the covers the old shopman appeared again. "You'd better not look at that book," he said. "That's a dangerous book. It's got *you* in it."

John was startled. "What do you mean?" he said.

"It's a queer book," said the old man. "Anyone who looks well into it will see himself in the future. I wouldn't look, if I were you. You might not like what you see."

"Why not?" asked John, puzzled. "I'm going to be a doctor. I'd like to see what I look like as a grown-up doctor. I'm going to be a clever doctor. I'm not only going to make people well, I'm going to make a lot of money, too."

"I wouldn't look in that book if I were you," said the old man, and he tried to take the book away. "Look here, my boy, I'm old and I know a lot. You've got a mouth that looks a bit hard to me. You've a wrinkle over your eyes that tells me you can be unkind. You've

21

"*I wouldn't look in that book,*" said the old man

a look in your eyes that tells me you don't always speak the truth. Don't you look into that book. You'll see something that will make you afraid and unhappy."

Well, that made John feel he simply must see the pages of that book. He couldn't really believe that they would show him himself, but he felt that he must find out.

"I want to see," he said. "Please, do let me see. I won't damage the book in any way."

He looked up at the old man and smiled. Now John's smile was very nice. His eyes lighted up, and creased at the corners, his mouth curved merrily, and his whole face changed. The old man looked at him closely.

"I believe you're half-and-half," he said. "If you are, this book will show you *two* stories with pictures – one story will begin at the beginning of the book. The other one you'll find by turning the book the other way and opening it at the end. If you're a half-and-half – that is, half-good and half-bad – there's no harm in letting you see the book. All right. Have your own way. We'll open the book at this end first."

The old man opened the book and John stared in great surprise – for there was a picture of himself, in jersey and shorts, just as he was then.

"You," said the old man, and turned a page. "Here you are doing something you're ashamed of – ah, yes – cheating at sums. Dear, dear, what a pity! And here you are boasting about something you hadn't really done. And look – what's this picture? You're bigger here – about two years older, I should think. You are telling an untruth without even going red! You're winning a prize, but only because you told that untruth."

23

"I don't like this book," said John, and he tried to close it. The old man stopped him.

"No. Once you've opened it, you've got to go on. Look at this picture – you're quite big here, you've got long trousers on. You're being unkind to a smaller boy – but there's no one to see, so you don't mind. Nasty little bully! And oh, look here – who's this? Your mother?"

"Yes," said John. "Why is she crying in the picture?"

"Because she's so disappointed in you," said the old man. "Look, it's her birthday – she's got a birthday-card in her hand. She wanted you to spend her birthday with her, and you had promised to – but at the last moment somebody asked you to go to a picnic and you went there instead. You didn't really mind if your mother was sad or not. She's thinking about you – feeling disappointed that you are growing up into a selfish, boastful, unkind youth."

"I don't like that picture," said John, in a trembling voice. "Turn the page, quick."

The page turned. "Why, here you're grown up!" said the old man. "Fine-looking fellow, too. You're studying to be a doctor. You said you meant to be one, didn't you? Well, you are going to be. This man here in the picture with you is saying that to be a doctor is a wonderful thing – you can bring healing and happiness to people who need it. But you are laughing and saying: 'That's all very well. I'll do that all right – but I'll be a rich man, too. I'll make people pay all I can.'"

John said nothing. He didn't like himself at all in the pictures. The old man turned to him. "You mustn't be surprised at what you see," he said gravely. "After all, you tell stories now – you are sometimes hard and unkind – you are not always honest and I can see you

24

are often selfish. Well, those things grow, my boy, they grow – and this is what they grow into!"

The pages turned again. John saw himself getting older and older. He saw himself getting rich. He saw himself with a pretty little wife – with merry children. He saw himself getting older still, and his face was not pleasant. It was hard and selfish.

He saw himself being pleasant to rich people, and rough with poor ones. He saw himself cheating when he could do it without being found out. He saw himself being bad-tempered at home, and unkind to the children. And then, alas, came some dreadful pictures, when he had been found out in some wrong-doing, and had lost all his money! His children left home when they were old enough, because they hated him – and his pretty little wife grew ugly and bad-tempered because she was lonely and unhappy.

"I hate this book!" cried John. The pictures had come to an end. The old man turned the book round the other way, and opened the pages from the end instead of at the beginning.

"Wait," he said. "I told you you were a half-and-half, didn't I? We'll see what the other half of you might lead to."

And there, page by page, was the story of what would be John's life if the good half of him grew, instead of the bad.

You should have seen those pictures! He won prizes, not by cheating, but by hard work. He gained friends, not by boasting, but by kindness. His mother smiled out from the story, happy in an unselfish and loving son. There he was, studying to be a doctor, but this time not boasting that he meant to be rich. This time he was saying something else. "The world is divided into two kinds of people – the ones who help and the ones who have to *be* helped. I'm going to be one who helps. I don't care if I make money or not – but I do care if I make happiness."

And there was his pretty little wife again – and his merry children. But this time they loved him, gave him a great welcome whenever he came home. They hadn't so much money – but how proud they were of John. How the sick people loved him, and how happy he was. His face was not so hard as in the other pictures. It was kind and merry. It was the face of a great and a good man.

"Well, there you are," said the old man, shutting the book up softly. "You're a half-and-half, as I said. Let the bad half of you grow, and it will grow into a bad man. Let the good half grow, and you'll get plenty of happiness and give it to others as well. Ah, my boy, there's a reason for not telling fibs, for not being dishonest, for not being unkind, for not cheating, for not being mean. We've all got the choice when we're small of letting one half of ourselves grow, or the other half. Nobody else but ourselves can choose."

"Yes," said John, in a small voice.

"You may think to yourself, 'Nobody knows I'm telling a fib,'" said the old man. "But *you* know it. That's what matters. It makes the wrong half grow, you see. Well, my boy, you'd better get back home now. And never mind about that work-basket. I can easily sell it to someone else if you haven't enough money."

"I *have* enough money," said John. "At least, I shall have tomorrow, when Daddy gives me my Saturday sixpence. That was really a fib I told. I wanted a knife, you see, that would cost three shillings. But now I am going

26

to spend the whole of my money on that basket for my mother's birthday."

"Take it with you now," said the old man, "and bring me the money tomorrow."

"Will you trust me, then?" asked John. "I told you a fib just now, you know."

"I'll trust you," said the old man. "Go along, little half-and-half. Here's the basket."

John went, full of wonder and very puzzled. A good many things were suddenly very clear to him. He saw now why it mattered so much whether he chose to do wrong things or right things. He had to make himself, good or bad. The man he was going to be would be exactly as he made him. It was the little things, the right and wrong things he did, that were going to lead to all sorts of big things.

That isn't quite the end of John's story. He's a great doctor now, the kindest, honestest, jolliest man you could meet. He says that the queer Enchanted Book told him things every child ought to know.

"Most children are half-and-half," he says. Well – I expect you are, too, aren't you? Choose the right half, whatever you do, and let it grow. I can't show you the Enchanted Book, because I don't know where it is now, but if ever I find it, we'll look at it together. I wonder what it will show us!

## Big-Eyes, The Frog

In the summer-time Big-Eyes, the frog, had a wonderful time. First he lived in the pond with all his brothers and sisters, aunts, uncles and cousins, and swam about and dived and croaked all day long.

Then he left the pond and found a very nice home for himself in a damp ditch. There was long grass in the ditch, and because the ditch was old and smelly, many flies came there. Big-Eyes liked flies for his dinner, and he grew very fat and strong.

"I wish I could catch flies with my tongue as you do!" said the robin, who lived in the hedge above. "I have to fly after them, and sometimes they are too quick for me. But all you do is to sit still in the grass, wait for a fly to buzz overhead – then you flick out your tongue quickly and catch the fly. It is marvellous to watch!"

The frog felt very clever. He swelled up a little and spoke in a croaking voice to the robin. "I have a wonderful tongue," he said, and he flicked it out for the robin to see. "It is fastened to the front of my mouth instead of to the back – so I can flick it out a long way of course! And, what is more, it is a nice sticky tongue, so that flies stick to it. Now, if you had a tongue like mine you would not need to waste your time flying after blue-bottles and daddy-long-legs. You could just sit and use your tongue!"

Just then a rat came slinking through the grass. It saw the fat frog and stopped. Big-Eyes saw the rat, too. At once he leapt high into the air, so high that the rat was very startled indeed. It gave a squeal and ran off.

"Well now, look at that!" said the robin, in admiration. "You can even frighten a rat, and goodness knows they are fierce enough creatures. How can you jump so high?"

Big-Eyes swelled himself up again. "I have very powerful hind legs," he said. "Oh, very powerful indeed. When I straighten them out suddenly they lift me high into the air. You should grow legs like mine, robin, then you would never need to be afraid of enemies!"

"I wish I could," said the robin, looking at his own thin little legs. "Still, I have my wings. I think really they are better than high-jumping legs."

"Indeed they are not," said the frog, but the robin had flown away. Big-Eyes sat in the ditch and thought of all the robin had said. He felt very grand. He was indeed a clever fellow. He could sit and catch his dinner without moving anything but his tongue. He could frighten even a fierce rat just by leaping into the air.

He set off to visit Crawler, the Toad, who lived under a stone nearby. "Good day," he said to Crawler. "It's a pity you haven't fine powerful back legs like mine. Poor creature, it must be dreadful to have to crawl along as you do."

"I don't pity myself, so there's no need for *you* to pity me," said Crawler snappily. "Getting a swelled head aren't you? Getting all vain and conceited? Go away. You'll be sorry some day if you think too much of yourself."

Big-Eyes leapt away. He soon met Spiky, the Hedgehog, and he spoke to him. "Why do you rush about as

29

you do, hurrying after grubs and beetles? Why don't you sit quietly like me, and let them come to you?"

"Oh, you're marvellous, aren't you!" said Spiky rudely. "I suppose you think that my dinner would come walking up to me each day. Frogs are stupid creatures."

"Indeed they are not," said Big-Eyes at once. "I can tell you this: I am about the cleverest frog that has ever lived. Even the robin thinks I am marvellous."

"Dear me! Well, you'd better ask the frogs to make you king!" said Spiky, and hurried away to find some slugs.

"Now that's rather a good idea," thought Big-Eyes. "I think I *will* tell the frogs to make me king. They haven't got a king, so why shouldn't I be their ruler? I am sure I am clever enough to rule well, and to make all kinds of laws."

On his way to the pond he met the dormouse. "I'm going to be made king of the frogs," he told the dormouse, proudly.

"Whatever for?" said Dozy, surprised. "I've always thought you such a stupid fellow!"

"Then you were quite wrong," said Big-Eyes. "I am very clever. I shall make all kinds of fine laws. You just see!"

"Well, no new laws for *me*!" said Dozy, and scurried away to find his favourite seeds.

Big-Eyes went on, leaping high. Red-Fur, the squirrel, saw him springing along, and ran down his tree to meet him.

"Hallo!" he said. "What are you doing leaping along in the open like that? You'll be seen by an enemy."

"I have already frightened the rat away," said Big-Eyes, squatting close to the ground. "I am not afraid of anyone. I am going to be king of the frogs."

30

Red-Fur laughed. "*You!*" he said. "Why, you are only an ordinary little frog, a little stupider than the others. Anyway, frogs are all stupid!"

"Why do you say that?" asked Big-Eyes, offended.

"Well, for one thing, what do you do all the winter?" said Red-Fur. "You stand on your heads in the mud at the bottom of the pond! A fine way to pass the winter, I must say. I never heard of anything so stupid in my life."

"Well, what do *you* do, then?" asked Big-Eyes.

"Oh, I am very clever," said Red-Fur. "*Really* clever! I save up plenty of nuts for myself, and hide them in corners. Then, when the cold weather comes I curl myself up in a nice cosy spot in a tree – not in the cold mud at the bottom of the pond – and there I wait till the cold weather goes. As soon as a warm spell comes I frisk out of my sleeping place and go to find my nuts. I don't waste all the winter days as you do."

"When I am king I shall make new laws," said Big-Eyes. "I shall order all frogs to put aside food for the winter, and I shall tell them to keep awake, and not to go to sleep in the pond. Then we shall be as clever as you."

"Impossible!" said Red-Fur, with a laugh, and bounded back up his tree.

Big-Eyes went to the pond and croaked loudly. He knew that most of his frog-friends lived round and about the pond in the wet grass and under the bushes. Soon they all answered him with loud croaks, and came out to see what he wanted.

"Frogs, I'm your king!" croaked Big-Eyes. "I shall make new laws, so that all the other creatures will know that frogs are clever, and not stupid. You will collect food for the winter days, so that you will not have to

31

sleep in the muddy pond when the cold weather comes. We will eat our stored food then, and hop about the fields and have a fine time."

"Be king if you like," said the frogs. "We don't mind!" And they all went back to their hiding-places.

"Well, now I'm king, really king," thought Big-Eyes, pleased. "It's true they didn't seem very pleased, and they didn't say they would obey my orders. Still, I'm king, and that's the main thing!"

He told everyone he was king. He made himself a crown of plaited grass. He felt very grand when a passing snail called him "Your Majesty".

The summer went. Autumn came. At first it was mild, but then came cold and frosty nights. The frogs all went to the pond and dived in. They swam to the mud at the bottom and cuddled there. They hated the frost, and they wanted to sleep and forget it.

Big-Eyes felt very cold. He wanted to store up food for himself, but there were no flies or grubs to be found now. The frost had killed them all. He felt hungry and miserable. He thought longingly of the pond, and going to sleep in the mud.

One day he could bear it no longer. He had had nothing to eat for four days. He was thin and freezing-cold. "I shall go to the pond. My laws were not so good after all," said Big-Eyes to himself, no longer feeling at all grand.

He hopped to the pond – but alas, there was a curious covering all over it that Big-Eyes had never in his life seen before! He sat and stared at it. He hopped out on to it. It was very cold. "Someone has put a lid on the pond!" he said.

He didn't know it was ice. He couldn't imagine what

32

Big-Eyes, the Frog, sat and stared at the pond

it was at all! He thought he would go and ask Crawler, the Toad, for help.

But Crawler was sound asleep and would not wake for weeks. So Big-Eyes hopped off to Spiky's hole in the bank.

But Spiky was fast asleep, curled up in his hole among dead leaves. He wasn't going to wake until the warm days came again!

Then Big-Eyes went to Dozy's home, a hole under the roots of a big pine tree. But it was no use croaking loudly to Dozy. He was curled up in a ball fast asleep, very fat and round. He wouldn't wake until the spring sunshine put warm fingers into his hole!

"This is dreadful!" said Big-Eyes, in despair. "All my friends are asleep. What shall I do? Oh, if only I could get into my pond. If only somebody would take the lid off and let me in! Why did I make myself king? It was because I was so stupid, not because I was so clever!"

He heard the pattering of paws and saw Red-Fur, the Squirrel.

"Hallo!" said Red-Fur. "Fancy seeing you on a winter's day! I'm just off to my hole in the tree. The weather is going to be colder, and I'm going to sleep until the warm days come again."

"Red-Fur, who has put that lid on the pond?" croaked poor Big-Eyes. "I want to get in and I can't."

Red-Fur laughed. "That's ice. It always comes in winter-time. It's not a lid. Nobody put it there. It just comes."

"But I want to get into the pond!" wailed poor Big-Eyes, half dead with cold.

"Well, let me see if I can help you," said Red-Fur

kindly. "There's a place just at the edge which isn't quite so hard. I'll see if I can make a hole for you."

So the squirrel took Big-Eyes to the edge of the pond, in a sheltered place, and scrabbled at the ice there. It was thin and broke quite easily.

"CRRRRRRRRROAK!" cried Big-Eyes in delight, and dived right underneath. He swam to the mud at the bottom and stood gladly on his head. He fell asleep. He was safe. He was doing what every frog should do in the winter-time. Now he wouldn't wake till the warm days came and the water was no longer covered with ice!"

"Silly little creature!" said Red-Fur, running up his tree. "Making himself king because he was so clever – and yet being stupid enough not to know he must sleep in the mud during the cold days. Well, well – it's what I've always said – squirrels are the cleverest creatures and frogs are the stupidest!"

He curled himself up and fell asleep. Only the rats and the rabbits, the stoats and the weasels were about then. It was sleeping-time. Big-Eyes slept as soundly as the others. I don't think he will wear a crown of plaited grass and call himself king next year, do you?

## The Surprising Sister

Jack was very cross with his sister Mary. She just wouldn't play Red Indians properly!

"I don't like you to catch me and shout in my ear!" she wailed. "You frighten me."

"You're a silly baby," said Jack.

Mary began to cry. "You always make me be the person who is caught," she sobbed. "If we play policemen and burglers I'm always the burgler, and you catch me and take me to prison. And if we play teachers and children I'm always the children and have to stand in the corner. It isn't fair."

"Well, you are the smallest, so you have to be what I say," said Jack. "Stop crying, for goodness' sake! How I wish I had a different sort of sister – one who never cries, but plays just how I'd like!"

And then a very queer thing happened. A little golden head peeped out of a nearby bush and looked at Jack. "Do you really wish that?" said the head.

Jack and Mary stared at the golden head in surprise. "Are you a fairy?" asked Mary, at last.

"Yes," said the golden head, nodding. "I live in this bush. I often watch the two of you play. Jack, would you really like another sort of sister?"

"Yes," said Jack. "Come out of the bush and let us see you."

Out of the bush climbed a fairy not much bigger than a doll. She had golden wings, and a little wand with a star at the end that glittered and shone.

"I can give you another sister if you like," said the fairy. "Mary, would you like to come to Fairyland to pay a visit there, whilst I get Jack another sister?"

"Oh, yes, please!" said Mary, her eyes shining brightly.

"Very well," said the fairy. "Now, what kind of a sister do you want, Jack?"

"Well, I don't want one like Mary, small and babyish, always crying when I say anything to her," said Jack. "I want a proper sister, big and strong like me, who never cries but can play all kinds of games well. I want one with plenty of ideas. Mary never has any! She's no good to play with at all."

Mary began to cry again.

"There you are!" said Jack, in disgust. "Always in tears!"

"Poor little girl," said the fairy, taking Mary's hand. "Never mind. You'll have a lovely time in Fairyland. Just wait for a moment whilst I get Jack the kind of sister he wants."

She drew a circle around her with her wand. She stepped inside and danced around, humming like a little top. Mary couldn't hear the words she hummed, but she knew they were magic because they sounded so queer.

And then, in the circle, someone else gradually came! At first she was only a mist – and then she seemed to get thicker and thicker, and at last the two surprised children saw that a girl was standing there, dressed in a red overall and red shoes and socks.

*She danced around, humming like a little top*

The fairy stopped humming. She jumped out of the circle, and the magic girl stepped out too. She was a big strong child, and she grinned widely at Jack.

"This is your new sister," said the fairy. "She will play with you as long as you like. If anything goes wrong whilst I am away with Mary, stand inside the magic circle here and call for me. My name is Peronel."

The fairy stepped inside the circle again and pulled Mary with her. She hummed the queer song and to Jack's amazement they both gradually disappeared. It was very strange to watch.

"What's your name?" asked the new sister.

"Jack. What's yours?" asked Jack.

"Matilda," said the girl.

"Not a very nice name," said Jack.

"Don't you say things like that to me!" said Matilda, looking suddenly fierce.

"Good gracious! Don't fly into a temper!" said Jack. "Mary never did that."

"Well, you wanted someone quite different from Mary, didn't you?" said Matilda. "Mary is sweet-tempered. I'm not. So look out!"

"Let's play Red Indians," said Jack. "Don't let's quarrel. Now – I'll be the Red Indian Brave coming to catch you. I shall jump out at you from behind a bush, and carry you off and tie you to a tree. That will be fun."

"Well, I think *I'll* be the Red Indian Brave," said Matilda firmly. "I don't much like being the prisoner. Now – look out, I'm coming. Go and hide from me. Oh – and I'll wear your feathered hat, I think. I shall feel more real then."

She snatched off Jack's Red Indian hat. He was cross and tried to grab it back. Matilda gave him a hard push that sent him to the ground.

"Don't do that," said Jack crossly. "Mary would never do a thing like that!"

"Well, I've told you before, I'm quite different from Mary," said Matilda, setting the Indian feathers on her head. "Now – you go and hide. Go on, or I'll push you again!"

Jack could do nothing but go and hide behind a bush. Matilda crept up softly. She suddenly leapt on Jack with the most terrible yell he had ever heard in his life!

"Ow – ee– ho – ee – EEE!" yelled Matilda. "Ow – ee – oh – ee – EEEE! I've got you! I've got you!"

"Don't deafen me like that," said Jack, "and don't hold me so hard. You're pinching my arm."

"Well, I'm a Red Indian, aren't I?" said Matilda. "I'm fierce and savage and strong. Listen to my war-whoop! Ow – ee – oh – ee – EEEE!"

"Be quiet!" said Jack, struggling hard. But Matilda was stronger than he was, and she dragged him over to a tree. She took some strong string from her pocket and tied him tightly to the trunk. He didn't like it at all. He had often done it to Mary, and she hadn't liked it much either.

"Now you're my prisoner and I'm going to dance all round you," said Matilda. "This is my Indian war-dance. You shall hear my war-song too."

Matilda did her dance and sang her song. Jack struggled with the string and at last got free. He shook away the string and went up to Matilda.

"Let's stop this silly game," he said. "Let's play something else. I'll choose."

"No, I'll choose," said Matilda at once.

"But I always do choose," said Jack. "Mary never had any good ideas for games, so I aways chose them."

"Well, I'm quite different from Mary – I keep telling you that," said Matilda. "I've got plenty of ideas. Heaps and heaps."

"Don't be selfish," said Jack. "Now look – let's play Ludo."

"*Ludo!*" said Matilda scornfully. "That's an indoors game. Don't be silly. If we're in the garden, we must play a garden game. We'll play – we'll play – doctors and patients."

"How do you play that?" asked Jack.

"Well, one of us has to be ill and go to bed, and the other one is the doctor," said Matilda. "And the doctor says what's the matter, and gives the patient medicine to make him better, and all sorts of things like that."

"I'll be the doctor," said Jack. "You can be ill and go to bed."

"Oh, no. *I'm* going to be the doctor," said Matilda, in a very firm voice. "It's my idea and my game. You've got to do what I tell you."

"Well I like that!" cried Jack, in a rage. "I'm a boy, aren't I? So I ought to be the doctor."

"There are women doctors, silly," said Matilda. "Fancy you not knowing that! What a baby you are!"

"I am not," said Jack, feeling very angry indeed.

"Well, *I* think you are, so there," said Matilda. "Now – this deck-chair is the bed. Lie down, please, and be ill. And be sure to be polite to me when I come to see you, because everybody is always polite to doctors."

"I am NOT going to be in bed and wait for you to come and see me," cried Jack. But Matilda took him by the arm and pushed him, bump, into the deck-chair. She was much stronger than he was – about as much stronger than Jack as Jack was stronger than Mary. He just had to do what he was told.

41

"Now stay there," said Matilda. "I'm going to be the doctor! Be careful I don't make you drink lots of nasty medicine!" Jack lay back in the deck-chair, thinking that his new sister wasn't at all a nice kind of girl. She was so rough, and wanted her own way too much. He didn't like to get out of the chair in case she pushed him down, bump, again.

Matilda came walking over to the chair, looking grave and serious. She looked down on Jack. "Good morning, little boy," she said. "I am sorry to hear that you are ill. What is the matter?"

"Oh, nothing much," said Jack. "I feel better already. I'll get up."

"Dear, dear, dear, what a way to talk to the doctor!" said Matilda, with a frown. "Let me feel your pulse and take your temperature."

She took hold of his left hand just as doctors do, and put a piece of grass into his mouth, pretending that it was a thermometer.

Then she took out the grass and looked at it. "Yes, you have got measles and chicken-pox and whooping-cough all at once," she said. "I must give you some medicine. Lie quite still, please."

"I don't want to lie still," said Jack. "This is a silly game. If we are going to play it *I'll* be the doctor." He sat up, meaning to get out of the deck chair, but Matilda gave him a sharp slap.

"Naughty boy! Lie still!"

"Matilda! Doctors are kind to their patients. They don't hit them," cried Jack.

"Well, you are a very bad patient, and I am not a good-tempered doctor," said Matilda. "So be careful! Now I am going to get you some medicine."

She went off and came back with a bottle and a little

42

glass. Jack couldn't imagine where she had got them from! She poured out half a glassful of strange red medicine. It bubbled as she poured it out.

"Now you drink that and your head will be better," she said.

"My head is quite all right, thank you," said Jack. "And I don't want the medicine. I shall pour it on the grass if you make me have it."

"Oh, what a naughty boy your are!" cried Matilda. "The worst patient a doctor could ever have. I am ashamed of you. Here is your medicine. Drink it all up."

Jack knocked the glass out of Matilda's hand and the red medicine spilt on the grass. Matilda flew into a rage. She slapped Jack so hard with her big strong hand that he yelled. Then she poured out a whole glassful of the medicine, and before he knew what she was doing, Matilda had emptied it all down his throat! She was so strong that he couldn't stop her!

"Oh! Oh!" spluttered poor Jack. "It's simply horrid! Oh, how could you give me medicine like that! It will make me worse, not better! Oh, you horrid girl!"

"I'm a doctor, not a girl," said Matilda. "Now you listen to me – you mustn't get up for a long time. I will come and give you some more medicine presently. This is a lovely game, isn't it?"

"It's a perfectly horrid game," said Jack. "I'm tired of being the patient. Let *me* be the doctor now. I'll give you some of that medicine."

He tried to get out of the chair, and Matilda pushed him back. The chair fell down beneath him, and poor Jack's fingers got trapped in it! How he yelled!

"Oh, my fingers!" he sobbed. "I've pinched them dreadfully in the chair."

"You *are* a cry-baby!" said Matilda, in disgust. "You really are! Cry-baby, cry-baby! What's the use of a brother like you, I should like to know? No fun at all! You don't play any games properly – and you cry at the least thing!"

"Oh, my poor fingers!" wept Jack. "You horrid girl! If you really *were* a doctor you would put them right again."

"Well, that's a good idea. I'll go on being a doctor," said Matilda, pleased. "I'll bind up your fingers."

She took Jack's hanky from his pocket and tore it into strips to make a bandage. Jack was very angry. His mother wouldn't like that at all. But it wasn't a bit of use saying anything to Matilda. She did exactly what she wanted and couldn't be stopped.

Matilda took Jack's pinched fingers in hers. He tried to snatch his hand away, because it hurt him to have his fingers touched. But Matilda snatched his hand back back and tied up his fingers so tightly that he sobbed with pain.

"Let me go! I don't want my hand bound up. You have made it worse, not better."

"You simply MUST do as the doctor tells you," said Matilda, enjoying herself thoroughly. "Now, go back to bed, and I will give you another sort of medicine."

"No, you won't!" cried Jack, and he pushed Matilda away. She pushed him too – and he went flying over the grass. He fell down with a bang – and then he saw that he was in the ring that the fairy had made on the grass with her little shining wand!

He remembered what the fairy had said – that if anything went wrong he was to go into the magic ring

44

and call her. Well – things had gone very wrong! He didn't like the new sister at all! He badly wanted gentle little Mary, who was always so willing to play his games. After all, Mary was two years younger than he was, and much smaller. He had often been horrid to her – just as horrid as Matilda had been to him. He wouldn't be any more, if only Matilda would go and Mary would come back!

Jack sat in the middle of the ring, with Matilda rushing over him, and yelled for the fairy.

"Peronel! Peronel! Peronel!"

And at once Peronel appeared in the ring beside him. Matilda stopped and stared.

"What's the matter?" asked Peronel, in surprise. "Don't you like your new sister? She is exactly what you asked for, you know. She can play games with you in just the same way that you made Mary play with you."

"Well, I don't like her a bit and I want Mary back," said Jack, wiping away some tears. "This horrid girl has made me into a cry-baby. She justs wants her own way all the time, and she isn't a bit kind at all. Please let me have Mary back."

"She may not want to come," said Peronel. "She has been having a lovely time in Fairyland, you know. Still, I will call her back and see if she would like to be your little sister again. If she would, I'll take Matilda away. But if she wouldn't, I'm afraid you'll have to keep Matilda."

Peronel waved her wand and hummed her magic song. Jack felt someone beside him – and there was Mary again. She looked at Jack in surprise.

45

"Jack! What's the matter? Why are you crying? You never cry! Have you hurt yourself? What's the matter with your poor hand?"

Jack felt two loving arms round his neck, and more tears came into his eyes. He gave Mary a hug.

"I'm awfully glad to see you," he said.

"Listen, Mary," said Peronel. "Jack doesn't seem to like the new sister I gave him, though she's a big strong girl, able to play all the games he wants, and has plenty of ideas of her own too. He seems to want you to come back. Now I know you are having a marvellous time in Fairyland, and I shan't make you stay with Jack unless you want to. You can choose. Fairyland is lovely – wouldn't you like to go back there? Jack will soon get used to Matilda."

Mary looked at Jack and smiled a little smile. "I'd rather stay with Jack, thank you," she said. "He is often cross with me and teases me, and makes me play games I don't want to – but if he's unhappy with Matilda, I'll comes back. It's not much good being a sister unless you are loving and kind, is it? I'll come back and be your little sister again if you really want me to, Jack."

"Oh, Mary – I do want you to so badly," said Jack, putting his arm round his sister. "I know now how you must have often felt, when I was rough and unkind. Come back and I'll just show you what a nice little sister I think you are! We'll play Red Indians – and you can be the Red Indian Brave. We'll play policemen and robbers – and you can be the policeman."

"Peronel, thank you for my lovely time in Fairyland," said Mary. "Please take Jack's new sister away."

Peronel waved her wand. Matilda went all misty – and then blew away like smoke from a chimney. It was

46

very queer. Then Peronel jumped back into the bush where she lived, and called good-bye.

"What a strange sort of adventure," said Jack. "I'm glad it's ended well, though. Oh, Mary – suppose I'd had to have Matilda for my sister always! What a dreadful time I would have had! Come along indoors and you shall choose the very biggest chocolate out of my chocolate box!"

## Greedy Gubbins

Gubbins was a fat puppy dog. He belonged to Freda, and they had great fun together. Gubbins was all white except for one ear and eye, and they were black. He had a long, wavy tail that wagged when he was pleased, and tucked itself between his back legs when he was sad.

Gubbins wasn't often sad. He was a greedy, merry little dog, who loved a game of ball, or a game of chew-the-slipper or shake-the-mat.

As he grew a bit he got hungrier and hungrier! He was always looking for food. He ran all round the house licking up any crumbs under the tables. He tried to put his front paws up on the table to sniff there, but he wasn't quite big enough. Then he discovered that he could jump on a chair, and from the chair get on to the table.

And then, tails and whiskers, what a feast he had! He tipped off the cover of a dish that smelt very good and ate up six sausages there!

Then he sat down in the middle of the table, his tongue hanging out, and his tail wagging so hard that one salt-cellar and one pepper-pot went flying from the table into a corner of the room!

Freda gave him a smacking for that. "You are getting too greedy for anything!" she said. "You have two good meals a day – so you shouldn't be hungry. But you are just greedy, Gubbins, I'm afraid – and I'm ashamed of you."

So after that Gubbins didn't get on the table any more, but tried to find somewhere else for food. It wasn't very long before he found the larder!

The cook had just put the joint of meat in there, and the smell came to Gubbins' nose. He sniffed in delight.

"Meat!" he thought. "That must be for me! Where has it been put?"

He trotted to find out, following the smell with his sharp nose. He came to the larder door. It was shut, so Gubbins lay down under the sink, and waited.

When the cook went to get butter from the larder, Gubbins slipped in beside her like a shadow. She didn't see him. He crept behind the door till she went out and shut it. Then Gubbins gave a tiny whine of joy. His meat was very near!

He tried to jump up to the shelf, but it was rather high. He jumped again – and just managed it. The meat was there, under his nose. My, it was good!

Gubbins began to chew the joint. The larder shelf was crowded with things, and he upset such a lot of them. He put one big paw into a dish of custard. He sat down on a plum pie. He upset a jug of milk – and that made the cook wonder whatever could be happening in her larder!

She ran to see – and when she saw Gubbins sitting on the shelf chewing the meat she *was* in a rage! She took a broomstick and gave Gubbins such a blow that he leapt off the shelf at once and ran howling into the garden. Freda ran to see what the matter was – but when she heard what the cook had to say, she was very angry indeed with Gubbins.

"You shall be tied up in your kennel," she said. "You are a thief-dog."

"Don't let him come into the house any more, Miss Freda!" called the cook. "He's spoilt and wasted I don't know how many things. Don't you let him indoors again. He must be made into an outdoor dog."

So after that Gubbins was not allowed indoors. He was very sad indeed – but it was no use. The cook shut the kitchen door firmly in his face every time he went there – and Freda pushed him outside if he tried to come in at the garden door.

"No, Gubbins," she said. "You are too greedy, you know. We don't trust you. We can't afford to have our food stolen by a naughty little dog who has two good meals of his own each day!"

Well, Gubbins now had to hunt round for food out-of-doors. He used to lie in wait for the tradesmen. He especially loved the butcher-boy, because he always smelt of meat, and he liked the fish-boy too.

One day the fish-boy left some fish in his bicycle-basket, whilst he went to take a chicken to the house. Gubbins smelt it. He put his paws against the bicycle and sniffed at the basket. Over went the bicycle! Out fell the fish!

Gubbins was thrilled. He tore off the wet paper and began to eat the fish. It *was* good!

But it wasn't quite so good when the fish-boy came out and threw a stone at Gubbins which hit him on the back and made him yelp!

"Don't throw stones at my dog," said Freda. "What has he done?"

"Well, Miss, he's eaten the fish that was in my basket," said the fish-boy angrily. "It'll have to be paid for."

So Freda had to take two shillings out of her money-box and pay for the fish. She was very cross with Gubbins.

"If you take anything else out of the baskets belonging to the tradespeople I shall give you a good whipping," she said.

Gubbins put his tail down and his ears went flat too. He was very sorry. He wouldn't do it again – only that fish did smell so good!

After that he didn't go near the bicycles of the errand-boys – but he ran round the shops! He went to the butcher's shop, hoping that the butcher would let a bit of meat fall – but the butcher chased him away every time, so he gave up going there. Then he went to the cake-shop, but the girl there had a pail of water which she threw at him as soon as his nose came round the door. So that wasn't any good, either. Then he went to the grocer's shop – but the grocer kept a very fierce and large black cat which had such an alarming hiss and such long claws that Gubbins felt he had much better keep away.

So now where could the greedy little puppy get food? He wasn't hungry, because Freda gave him bigger meals – but he was still greedy, and wanted to eat and eat even though he was not hungry.

Ah! the dustbin, of course! Exciting things were thrown away in dustbins! bones went there – and the scrapings of the stock-pot where the soup was made.

"I'll hunt in the dustbin as nobody seems to welcome me in the shops," thought Gubbins. So he visited the dustbin. It was rather high. He couldn't reach the top. What was he to do? The lid was on, too – that would be difficult to get off.

Then Gubbins found that he could work off the dust-bin lid with his black nose! If he stood up, his nose would just reach the lid – and he pushed and pushed until it slid off with a clang!

Now he only just had to jump into the dustbin. He went back a little way – ran hard, jumped – and right into the dustbin he sprang. Good!

What a mixture of things was there! Bones, peelings, skins, cinders – good gracious, Gubbins could have a wonderful time scraping about.

He heard somebody coming. He crouched down and tried to make himself as small as possible. The cook came up and emptied a sink-basket full of tea-leaves into the dustbin. They went all over Gubbins!

"Dear me!" said the cook, "there's the dustbin lid left off. Isn't that careless! The flies will come along and lay their eggs in the rubbish if the lid is left off!"

She picked up the lid and banged it on the dustbin. Gubbins was rather frightened, because quite suddenly he found himself in the dark! He didn't like it at all.

The cook went back to the kitchen. Gubbins pushed at the lid with his head – but this time the cook really had put the lid on tightly – and it couldn't be moved.

"I'll jump out the next time someone comes and takes the lid off," thought Gubbins, trying to lick the tea-leaves off his legs. "What a horrid taste these tea-leaves have!"

Suddenly a man walked into the yard, took off the lid, and hoisted the dustbin on to his back! Tails and whiskers, what a shock for Gubbins! He didn't dare to jump out because he was now too far from the ground.

It was the dustman! It was his day for taking the

*Gubbins sprang right into the dustbin*

rubbish, and *he* didn't know there was a dog inside the bin he was carrying! He just thought that the dustbin was a bit heavier than usual!

He carried the dustbin to his dust-cart. He climbed up the little ladder hanging over the side. He tipped up the dustbin and emptied it into the cart. He pulled down the great lid that covered up the dust and rubbish from the wind, and then, whistling loudly, put the empty dustbin back into the yard.

Gubbins was emptied into the dust-cart with the rubbish! He was frightened almost out of his skin. He lay on the great pile of rubbish, trembling and scared, not at all liking the different smells around him!

The cart moved off. Gubbins went with it. He began to whine, and the dustmen looked at each other in surprise.

"Funny noise the rubbish is making today," said one dustman.

"Yes – sort of whining," said the other. "Anyone might think there was a dog in there!"

They laughed. "Well, nobody would put a dog into a dustbin," said the first man.

Gubbins began to bark. The dustmen were more astonished than ever.

"The rubbish is barking now!" said one man. "I can't understand it!" He lifted up the great lid that covered half the dust-cart and looked inside. At once Gubbins leapt out, covered with potato peel, tea-leaves, dust, broken crockery, dead flowers and goodness knows what!

He didn't look like a dog at all! The dustman was scared. "I say, Bill, did you see that bit of rubbish jumping out?" he asked. "Seemed to me to have got legs!"

The dustmen shut the dust-cart again and went on their way, very puzzled. Gubbins tore home as fast as he could, frightened and unhappy. His mistress was most astonished to see him coming in all covered with rubbish!

"You look as if you've been in a dustbin, you dirty little dog!" she cried. "I'm ashamed of you! You must have a bath, because you smell so dreadful!"

Gubbins hated baths – but he had to have one because he smelt so bad. As he stood in the soapy water, whining miserably, he made up his little doggy mind that he wouldn't be greedy any more.

"I'll never tell anyone how I got shut in a dustbin!" he thought. And he never did. But the next-door cat had been on the wall when it happened, and had seen everything. So you may be sure *she* soon spread the news around – and wherever poor Gubbins went, a cat or a dog called out to him very rudely:

"Hallo, dustbin dog! Had enough to eat today?" Then Gubbins puts his tail down and trots away, ashamed. It really was a dreadful thing to happen, wasn't it?

## The Toy Telephone

John had a toy telephone for his birthday. It was just like a real one, but the only thing wrong with it was that when John picked up the receiver and spoke into it, nobody answered him.

So he had to speak for himself and for the person he was speaking to as well. Sometimes he rang up the dog next door, and sometimes he rang up the milkman's horse, and often he rang up all his friends and pretended to ask them to a party.

The telephone was green, and had a place to speak into and a place to listen at. It stood on the table where John's farm was set out, and looked very grand and grown-up.

One night a very strange thing happened. John was in bed, half-asleep, when he heard the sound of little high voices in the nursery next to his bedroom. At first he thought he must be dreaming, then he knew he wasn't because he could hear the wind and the rain so clearly against the window.

"It surely can't be my *toys* that are talking together!" said John, feeling excited. "No, it surely can't."

He sat up in bed and listened. Yes, there was no doubt about it at all – there *were* people talking in the nursery, and they had high bird-like voices, very sweet to listen to.

"I'm going to see who's there," said John. He slipped on his dressing-gown and crept to the door. He went to the nursery and peeped in to see who was there, expecting to see his toys playing about.

But the toys were all exactly as he had left them! Most of them were in the toy-cupboard, his teddy was in the arm-chair, and the farmyard was set out on the little table where the telephone stood.

John stared round the room. The fire was flickering, and it wasn't difficult to see. And then John saw something rather surprising!

Sitting on the hearthrug, drying themselves, were four tiny creatures with wings. They were talking together in bird-like voices, and John stared at them in the greatest surprise. At first he thought they were big moths, but soon he saw that they were pixies.

"I say!" he said, going right into the room. "I say! Who *are* you?"

The pixies sprang to their feet. But when they saw John's delighted face, they smiled up at him.

"We are four pixies, caught out in the rain," said one, in a voice like a robin's, creamy and high. "We flew in at the window to get dry. We *are* dry now – but we don't know whether to start out again or not, because if it goes on raining we shall get soaked. And Twinky here as already sneezed three times."

Twinky sneezed a fourth time, and the other pixies looked at him anxiously.

"I suppose you aren't any good at telling the weather, are you?" asked Twinky. John shook his head.

"No," he said. "I can never seem to tell if it is going to be fine or wet. If our gardener were here, he could tell you, but he isn't. He always knows the weather."

"Perhaps he knows the weather-clerk," said Twinky. "The weather-clerk lives up in the sky, you know, and always knows what weather is coming. I shouldn't be surprised if your gardener is friends with him."

"I don't think so," said John, rather astonished. "True, he always *does* look up at the sky when he tells me what the weather is going to be – but he has never said anything to me about the weather-clerk!"

"I wish we could telephone to the weather-clerk," sighed Twinky. "Then we should know what the weather will be for the rest of the night. We should know whether to stay here or whether to go on."

John suddenly remembered his toy telephone. He reached it down from the table. "Look!" he said. "Here's a telephone! It's my own. You can use it if you like. But I must tell you that although it's easy to speak into it, it is very, very difficult to hear anyone talking back to you."

"Oh, we can easily get on to the weather-clerk by using a little magic!" cried Twinky, sneezing again. He rubbed the telephone all over with his tiny handkerchief and then spoke into it.

"Hallo! Hallo! Is that the weather-clerk? It is? Good! Then listen, Weather-clerk. This is Twinky, the pixie speaking. It's just this minute stopped raining. Is it going to rain or blow any more tonight? If it isn't we can set out again in safety, and go home."

John heard a tiny voice talking back down the telephone, but he couldn't hear what it said. Twinky heard though, and nodded round to the others. "It's all right," he said. "We can go. There'll be no more rain to-

*"Hello, hello, is that the weather clerk?"*

night. Good-bye John. And thank you so much for letting us use your telephone!"

Before John could say more than good-bye, the four tiny creatures flew out of the window and were gone in the dark night. John looked at his telephone. He picked up the receiver and spoke softly into it.

"Are you there still, Weather-clerk? Is it going to be fine tomorrow, because I want to have a picnic?"

A tiny voice answered him from far away. "Yes, it will be fine tomorrow. You can have your picnic?"

"Oh, thank you!" said John joyfully, and crept back to bed. Sure enough the weather-clerk was right, and it *was* fine all the next day. And do you know, John *always* knows exactly what the weather is going to be, and I can guess why. It's because he can speak to the weather-clerk on his toy telephone whenever he wants to. Dear me, don't I wish he would lend it to me just for two minutes!

## Red Button Land

Harry and Lucy lived in Garage Cottage with their father and mother. Their father mended motor-cars and lorries all day long in his garage, so Harry and Lucy knew a lot about them. Harry wanted to have a little car of his own as soon as ever he was old enough – but as he was only eight he would have a long time to wait!

One very fine day their mother sent them to Cuckoo Wood for a picnic. She packed up sandwiches, buns and bananas for them, told them to be sure not to leave the paper and peel about in the woods, and to come home at six o'clock that evening. So off they went, feeling very happy and gay.

The sun shone down hotly, and the birds sang. It was a long way to Cuckoo Wood but the children didn't mind a bit. They meant to explore the wood and find out what was in the middle of it. It was a big wood, mysterious and dim in the middle parts, and both the children thought there might be brownies or witches there.

At last they got there. They were hungry, so they sat down and feasted on their lunch. Then they followed the little path that led to the centre of the wood.

"I hope we shan't get lost," said Lucy.

"I've got my compass with me," said Harry. "We shall be all right."

"The path really seems to be nothing but a rabbit-path now," said Lucy. "It's so narrow and hardly worn at all."

They went on and on. The wood grew thicker, and the leaves were so dense that the sunlight could no longer peep through them. It was dark and mysterious!

Suddenly the children came to a little clearing. No trees grew there, and no bushes – there was only smooth grass. And right in the middle of the grass was – what do you think? Why, a little aeroplane, not much bigger than a motor-car! It was painted yellow and blue, and it had two seats.

It was empty. Nobody was in the aeroplane at all. The children looked round to see who it belonged to – but they could see no one. Then Lucy saw a tiny cottage between the trees, and she pointed to it.

"Look, Harry! The airman must have landed here to see someone in that cottage. He'll be going away soon, so shall we wait here and see what he's like? It's such a funny aeroplane that I'm sure it belongs to one of the pixie folk!"

"I wonder how it works," said Harry, who was always wanting to know how things worked. He peeped inside the aeroplane – but to his great astonishment there didn't seem to be any handles, levers, knobs or anything else! He couldn't see how the aeroplane was driven at all.

"Well, that's funny!" he said. "I wonder how it goes. I'm going to get into the driver's seat, Lucy, to see if I can find out how the aeroplane is driven."

"Well, I'll get into the passenger's seat, then," said Lucy. "I'll pretend you're going to drive me up in the sky!"

She climbed into the little back seat; and Harry

climbed into the front one – but still he couldn't see anything to make the aeroplane go! It was very strange.

And then a very curious thing happened – the green propeller in front began to go round by itself, and before the children knew what was happening, the aeroplane took a little run forward, rose into the air and flew off over the trees!

Well! What a surprising thing! Harry and Lucy held on to their seats in astonishment and fright. They had never flown before, and it felt rather funny. They looked down. How small the fields and woods seemed! Just like toy ones – and the houses looked like dolls' houses.

"I say, Lucy! This is a fine thing to happen!" shouted Harry. "What are we to do?"

"We can't do anything, can we?" shouted back Lucy. "We don't know how to fly it – and anyhow, it's flying itself, so we can't stop it!"

"I wonder where it will take us!" shouted Harry. The wind made such a noise whistling past his ears that he had to shout to make himself heard.

Lucy shook her head. She was frightened. She wished they hadn't climbed into the aeroplane. Mother was always telling them not to meddle with things – and this was their punishment for meddling!

On and on the aeroplane went, over hills and valleys, fields and towns. At last, in the distance, Harry spied a shining, glittering city of pointed towers and silvery castles. Nearer and nearer it came, a beautiful city, and the children leaned over the side to look at it.

"The aeroplane's going down to it!" cried Harry suddenly. Sure enough it was – it dipped its blunt nose downwards and made straight for a wide, open place in the middle of the city. It landed with a bump and stood quite still.

Up ran a crowd of little men with pointed hats and shoes, big smiling faces and red buttons all down their brown tunics.

"Welcome back, welcome back, dear Wumple!" they cried – and then they discovered that dear Wumple was not in the aeroplane, but that two children were there instead! What a surprise they got! The smiles slid off their faces and they frowned.

"Where's Wumple?" they cried. "Where's Wumple? What have you done with Wumple?"

"Nothing," said Harry, climbing out of the aeroplane. "We don't even know who Wumple is. We found this aeroplane in Cuckoo Wood, and we climbed in to have a look at it – and it flew off with us! Where are we?"

"You are in Shining City, where the Red Button Folk live," said a fat little fellow, with very big buttons. "This is a very serious thing! You have stolen the aeroplane from Wumple."

"No, we didn't," said Lucy. "The aeroplane stole us! It flew off with us without even asking where we wanted to go."

"Nonsense, nonsense!" cried the Red Button Folk together. "You are talking nonsense. We must take you to our King and see what punishment you must have. Perhaps he will turn you into ladybirds or change you into mushrooms."

Lucy began to cry. Harry looked very fierce.

"If your King tries any tricks with us I shall change him into a worm and make him go into a hole!" he said boldly.

The Red Button Folk began to cry out at this, and they took hold of the two children and marched them off. They went to a corner, and there the children saw some little carriages drawn by big white rabbits. The Red Buttons bundled the children into two of the carriages, and then set off at a gallop.

"Where are we going?" asked Harry.

"To the King's palace!" said the biggest Red Button. What a pace they went! The dust flew up behind the rabbits' paws, and the little carriages rocked from side to side. At last they came to a marvellous building. It was built of silver and glass, and was so dazzling, that the children could hardly bear to look at it.

Everyone got out of the rabbit carriages, and the Red Button Folk ran the children up a long flight of glittering silver steps. At the top were two soldiers in yellow uniforms with red buttons all down their chests and all down their trousers, too.

"We want to see the King!" cried the Red Button Folk.

"You can't," said the soldiers. "He's gone out in his new car."

"Well, we'll wait then," said the Red Buttons, and they all trooped into the palace. The children looked round. The chairs and tables had glass tops and silver legs. The pictures had silver frames, and the floor was laid with a carpet of shining silver threads. It was all very beautiful and strange, but most dazzling.

"What make is the King's new car?" asked Harry, who always wanted to know everything about cars. "Is it a magic one, like the aeroplane?"

"Oh, no!" said one of the Red Buttons. "It's a real,

65

proper car, and it came from your world. Nobody knows how to drive it but Tipkins, who had a lesson at the place where it came from. Oh, it's a grand car!"

"What make is it?" asked Harry again. "Is it a Rolls-Royce or a Morris or what?"

The Red Buttons didn't know what Harry was talking about, and they shook their heads. Then one of them yawned and said he was hungry and thirsty.

"The bun-tree is flowering in the garden," said a nearby soldier. "And if you like, I'll turn on the lemonade fountain for you."

"Oh, thank you so much!" cried all the Red Buttons, and they rushed out into the garden through a big silver door, taking the children with them. What a wonderful garden it was! The children had never seen so many bright flowers before! Even the grass had little blue flowers, and seemed like a bright carpet.

In one corner was a queer tree. The children went up to it with the Red Buttons, and to their great surprise they saw that instead of flowers, currant buns were growing on it!

"Some are quite ripe!" cried one of the Red Buttons. "Pick them!"

They picked a large bun each, Harry and Lucy, too. How lovely they tasted! Then they all went to a fountain not far off and held out little tin mugs to the water ... but it wasn't water, it was lemonade!

The little Red Buttons were greedy. They went back to the bun-tree and picked a great many more buns. The sun was hot in the garden, and they sat on the grass and ate and ate. Soon they felt sleepy, and one by one they nodded their heads and fell asleep. Only Harry

66

and Lucy, who had not had more than one bun each, did not fall asleep.

"Greedy things!" whispered Lucy to Harry. "They've overeaten themselves like Puss does at home, and they've fallen asleep!"

"Let's run while we've got the chance!" said Harry, getting up. "Sh! Don't wake any of them!"

The children stepped carefully over the sleeping little men, and ran down the garden. After a long run they came to a high wall. In it was a green door. They opened it and found themselves in a lane.

"Good! Perhaps we can find someone who will show us the way back home!" said Lucy.

"It would be a long way to walk," said Harry. "I don't think we *could* walk so far, Lucy – do you?"

"Well, perhaps there's a train or something we could take," said the little girl, stepping out bravely. They went quickly up the lane, and soon came to a stile leading over a field. They climbed over it and found themselves in a field of yellow buttercups. They walked across field after field, and then came to a steep hill. At the top was a cottage, its curtains blowing in the breeze.

An old woman, very like a witch, was at the door shaking a duster.

"Could you tell us how to get to the village of Hayton?" asked Harry, politely. Hayton was where the two children lived.

"Hayton?" said the old dame, puzzled. "Never heard of it! It isn't in Fairyland, that I *do* know!"

"Goodness! Is this Fairyland?" asked Lucy, startled.

"Of course it is," said the old woman. "This is Red Button Land, part of the west of Fairyland. How did you get here?"

The children didn't want to tell her about the aeroplane in case she said they had stolen it, as the Red Buttons had said – so they simply said good-bye and turned to go. But she ran after them shouting:

"You come back! You come back! I've got a job for you to do!"

"Run! She's a witch!" cried Harry. The children ran as fast as their feet would take them, and didn't stop until the cottage was quite out of sight.

"Let's have a rest for a minute!" said Lucy, puffing and panting. "The old woman is quite left behind."

So they sat down by a hedge to get their breath – and whilst they were sitting there they heard a great many voices, all talking at once, on the other side of the hedge.

"What's the matter? Why won't it go?"

"Oh, what a nuisance this is!"

"Have we got to stay here all night, that's what *I'd* like to know?"

"I thought you said you *knew* how to work it?"

"What a dreadful noise!" whispered Lucy. "Let's peep through the hedge and see what's the matter."

They peeped through – and what a funny sight they saw! In the lane beyond was a motor-car – such a strange one! It was painted red with white spots all over it, and all round the doors were rows of red buttons. It had a hood like a big sunshade and inside sat a very grand person indeed, with two others. Outside, peeping under the bonnet of the car, was the driver, and he looked very worried.

68

"It must be the King of Red Buttons and his new motor-car!" whispered Harry. "What a funny car! Look at the red buttons all over it! And isn't the King cross!"

He certainly was. He banged on the seat with his hand, and shouted to the driver again.

"Why don't you make it go? You said you knew all about it! Am I to stay here all day? I never heard of such a thing in my life."

"Your Majesty, I'm very sorry," said Tipkins the driver, red in the face. "I'm afraid I can't make the car go. You'll have to walk home to the palace."

"WALK!" shouted the King in a rage. "WALK! All those miles! What are you talking about! You must be mad. Make the car go at once or I'll turn you into a red-spotted ladybird!"

The poor driver! He didn't know what to do and the children were quite sorry for him. Harry whispered to Lucy.

"I believe we might find out what's the matter, Lucy. We've watched Daddy mend cars often enough. Let's go and try. I couldn't bear to see that poor Red Button driver turned into a ladybird."

So the children scrambled through the hedge and appeared suddenly before the King. He was most surprised.

"Your Majesty," said Harry, saluting like a Boy Scout, "may I help you? I know a lot about cars."

"Where do you come from?" asked the King in astonishment. "I didn't know there were any children in Red Button Land."

"Oh, we just came here," said Harry, anxious not to

69

*"Your Majesty," said Harry, saluting, "may I help you?"*

talk about the aeroplane. "Now then, let's have a look at the car. Is there plenty of petrol?"

"Yes, plenty," said the driver. Harry looked at the car. Everything seemed to be all right. Suddenly something came into his mind. He climbed into the driver's seat, and looked at the brakes. They were on! So, of course, the car couldn't possibly move!

"Did you stop here for lunch?" asked Harry.

"Yes," said the King. "And when we got back into the car it wouldn't go!"

"It wouldn't go because you forgot to take off the brakes when you tried to start!" said Harry, laughing. "See, I'll take them off, and you'll find the car goes quite all right!"

He slid off the brakes, and when he pressed the starting knob, and did one or two other little things that he had seen his father do when driving a car, sure enough it started quite well! How pleased the King was!

"You shall drive me home!" he cried to Harry. "Yes, you shall. You are the cleverest boy I've ever met!"

"I haven't a driving-licence," said Harry.

"Oh, you don't need driving-licences in Fairyland," said the King. "Anybody can do anything. Get in, little girl, and your brother shall drive us to the palace. Driver, you can sit on the luggage grid."

Well, off they went – and didn't Harry feel proud! I should think so! He drove very carefully and very well, and hooted loudly at the corners. At last they arrived at the Palace, and drew up in great style.

Out came all the little Red Buttons who had captured the children that morning . . . but when they saw Harry and Lucy in the car they fell back, astonished.

"There are those wicked children who stole Wumple's aeroplane!" cried the biggest Red Button.

"Sh!" cried another. "They are friends of the King, look! One of them is driving. He must be very clever. Sh! Don't say anything!"

How glad the children were when the Red Buttons said never a word to the King about the aeroplane! They went into the Palace with him, and he ordered a magnificent tea – seventeen different kinds of jam, twenty-one different kinds of cakes, and six sorts of jelly. It certainly was a good tea.

"Now, let me run you home in my new car," said the King, kindly. "Or would you like to drive the car yourself, Harry? My own driver can bring it back – if only he doesn't forget to take off the brakes!"

So off they started after tea. Harry drove the car again and he did feel so proud. Lucy sat at the back with His Majesty, and he talked all the time about magic, so that she had a most exciting time. The driver sat beside Harry and watched all he did.

How everyone stared when Harry drove through his home village with the Red Button King at the back of the car, the big sunshade held over him, and with red buttons all over the doors. They couldn't believe their eyes!

Harry stopped at his house, Garage Cottage. He got out and so did Lucy. "Just wait a moment," he said to the King. "I'm sure my mother would like to see you."

He ran indoors with Lucy, longing to tell his mother of their grand adventure, and to show her the Red Button King. He found her in the kitchen making jam.

"Quick, Mother, come and see the Red Button King

from Fairyland!" he cried. "Quick! I drove him all the way home from Red Button Land."

Mother rushed out to the gate – but alas, His Majesty had felt shy and hadn't liked to wait. The car was half-way down the road, the big sunshade bobbing up and down as it went.

The King turned round and waved his hand. "Come back!" cried the children – but he shook his head.

"Bring your mother to see me next week!" he called back.

But, of course, Harry and Lucy don't know the way! The king had told them how to get home from Red Button Land – but they couldn't possibly find their way back alone! And they can't see Red Button Land on any of their maps, although they have looked all through their atlases. Isn't it a pity?

If ever you see Red Button Land printed on a map, do let me know, won't you? I could tell Harry and Lucy, you see.

## Clever Old Green-Eyes

Green-Eyes belonged to Morris. She was a big black cat, with a thick, silky coat, and the greenest eyes you ever saw.

"They are as green as the cucumbers you buy in the summer, Mummy," said Morris. "I do love Green-Eyes. She purrs so loudly, and she loves sitting on my knee. She is the nicest cat in the world."

Morris bought Green-Eyes a fine Christmas present. It was a cat-basket, made of wicker-work. Morris begged an old cushion from his mother, and an old bit of blanket. Then he picked up Green-Eyes and sat her down in the basket.

"It's yours, Green-Eyes, with my love," said Morris. "Mummy, may I have Green-Eyes' basket in my bedroom, please? Do let me. She is very good, and she won't make my room untidy or smelly at all, I promise you."

Well, Mummy didn't very much like a cat sleeping in Morris's room, but certainly Green-Eyes was a very good, quiet cat – so she said yes.

And, in great delight, Morris carried the basket up to his own little bedroom, with Green-Eyes following at his heels.

"There," he said to Green-Eyes, "you can sleep in my bedroom every night now, Green-Eyes – you in your basket and I in my bed. I will always leave the window open a little way, so that you can come in and out as you want to. You can easily scramble up the tree out-

74

side, and come in through the window if you are not in your basket when I have to go to bed." Green-Eyes was delighted. She purred loudly.

"Thank you, Morris. It is a very lovely basket and I like it very much. You are a kind little boy."

For three or four months Green-Eyes slept in her basket in Morris's bedroom – and then one morning Morris gave such a yell of surprise and delight that his mother came running to see what was the matter.

"Mummy, oh Mummy! Green-Eyes has laid four tiny little kittens in her basket! Oh, Mummy, we've got kittens. Isn't it exciting?"

"Very exciting," said Mummy. "But Green-Eyes will have to go to the barn now, Morris. I can't have five cats in your bedroom."

"Oh, Mummy – but four of them are only tiny kittens!" said Morris, almost in tears. "Mummy, Green-Eyes is so *used* to sleeping in my room now – she loves it. Don't make her unhappy by turning her out just when she's got four dear little kittens to look after. They will be safe with me. The rats might get them out in the barn."

"Dear me, Green-Eyes will certainly see that they don't!" said Mummy. "She has killed a good many rats in her time. No, Morris dear – she and her kittens must go to the barn. There is plenty of straw there to make her a nice soft bed. She will be very happy there."

"She will miss me so at night," said Morris. "And I shall miss her, too."

But Mummy was quite firm about it. Green-Eyes had got to go to the barn with all her kittens, and go she did. Mummy picked up the kittens, which squealed loudly. She went downstairs with them, and Green-Eyes followed at once.

75

Mummy took the four tiny kittens to the barn. They were all as black as could be, just like Green-Eyes. One of them had tiny white feet. It was sweet.

Green-Eyes made a bed for them in the straw and lay down. Mummy gave her the kittens, and they nestled up to her, asking her for some milk. Green-Eyes purred loudly.

"There, you see!" said Mummy to Morris. "Green-Eyes is quite happy."

But when night-time came, and Morris looked at the empty basket, he felt sure that Green-Eyes wasn't at all happy. Then he heard a little soft jump, and there was Green-Eyes in his bedroom, looking up at him.

"Oh, Green-Eyes – are you missing me? Are you missing your basket?" said Morris. "Mummy doesn't want your nice basket out in the barn. She says straw will be all right for you and the kittens. Let me stroke you. There now, go back to your kittens, and don't be miserable because you've been turned out!"

The kittens grew well, out in the barn. Their eyes opened and were very blue. Mummy said they would turn green later on. Soon they were able to creep out of the straw and play about a little. Morris loved them – but he still wished he could have them indoors!

One night about four weeks after the kittens had been born, Morris woke with a jump. His window was shut, and something was knocking against it. Thud, thud, thud, went the knocking, very soft and slow. Green-Eyes jumped inside, carrying a kitten by the skin at the back of its neck, the way all mother-cats carry their kittens. She dropped it into the basket nearby, gave a tiny mew, and then sprang out of the window and down the tree.

Morris was astonished. "Green-Eyes! What are you doing? Why have you brought your kittens here?"

Soon the cat was back with yet another kitten. Morris was more astonished than ever. What could Green-Eyes be doing? Was she tired of the barn? Had she suddenly taken it into her head to bring her kittens to the place that she herself liked so much? It was all very puzzling.

Then Morris smelt something funny – smoke! He sniffed and sniffed. Yes – it *was* smoke. But what smoke could it be? There was no bonfire burning, he knew that.

He slipped downstairs, just as Green-Eyes jumped in at the window, with her third kitten in her mouth. He ran out of the garden-door and went to the barn. Smoke was coming out of it!

"Fire! Fire!" yelled Morris. "Mummy! Daddy! The barn's on fire! Quick, quick!"

He saw Green-Eyes come out of the smoking barn, dragging her last kitten in her mouth.

"Oh, you good, clever little cat!" he said. "You have saved all your kittens by yourself! And perhaps you will have saved our barn, too, if only Mummy and Daddy come quickly enough."

It wasn't very long before a crowd of grown-ups were hosing the smoking barn with water. Inside, fast asleep, was an old tramp. He had lit a candle there and fallen asleep before putting it out. It had burned down, set the straw alight, and set fire to the big barn.

Soon the fire was out. The tramp was rubbing his eyes in amazement, and Morris was telling everyone about Green-Eyes.

*"Fire! Fire!" yelled Morris*

"She brought her kittens to my bedroom, where her old basket is, and that's what woke me. I went out and saw the barn on fire. Mummy, Daddy, Green-Eyes saved the barn – and saved the life of that old tramp, too!"

They all went back to bed, happy and excited. Mummy peeped into Morris's room and smiled.

"Well, well, I suppose I'll have to let you have Green-Eyes and all the kittens there now, Morris. She saved our barn for us, so I must give her a reward!"

So Green-Eyes slept in the basket with her four kittens, and Morris was very happy. But when they were six weeks old they woke him up every morning by clambering on to his bed and nibbling his nose. So, in the end, he had to take them down to the kitchen!

"As soon as they go to their new homes you can come back to my bedroom and sleep in your basket," he told Green-Eyes. "You'll like that, won't you?"

"Purrrrr-rrr-rrr," said Green-Eyes, and Morris knew what *that* meant.

## She Didn't Want To Go

Sheila was a lazy little girl, who never wanted to go for a walk, and wouldn't run unless she had to. So she grew rather fat and ugly, and wasn't very good-tempered.

The other children used to call to her as they went by on their way to walk in the woods and the hills.

"Sheila! Come along, lazy-bones! It's such a lovely day, you'll love a walk!'"

But Sheila wouldn't go. She sat in the garden with a book, and grumbled so much even when her mother wanted her to run to the post, that soon nobody asked her to run any errand at all.

When the children came back from their walk they would call to Sheila again.

"Sheila! Look at the flowers we've got! And do you know, we found some wild strawberries! And oh, Sheila, we saw a little red squirrel running up a tree!'"

"Really?" Sheila would say with a yawn. "Goodness, how dusty your shoes are! You must have walked for miles! I can't imagine why you bother when you can sit at home in the garden and laze in the sunshine."

"You'll turn into a big old tabby-cat one day!" said the children. "We'll see you lying asleep in the sun on the wall, with your tail hanging down!"

"Don't be so rude!" said Sheila, and turned to her book with a frown.

Now one day Sheila went out to a birthday party. Every child was given a balloon, and Sheila's was the most beautiful of all. It was half blue and half yellow, and was simply enormous. Sheila was delighted with it. She went home to show her mother and the balloon bobbed behind her on its string.

All the children in the street cried out in wonder at the sight of Sheila's balloon. "Look! Look at that balloon! Isn't it marvellous!"

Sheila was proud. She took her balloon indoors and her mother liked it as much as she did. "You can hang it up in your bedroom," said her mother. "Then you can see it as soon as you wake up."

So that night Sheila hung her balloon up in her room, and in the morning the sun shone on it and made it gleam like a great big bubble. Sheila took it downstairs with her. It was Saturday and there was no school.

"I shall play with my lovely balloon in the garden," said the little girl. "There is a nice breeze blowing and the balloon will fly beautifully. I shall be very careful not to let it touch the prickly holly-bush though."

Down the garden she went with her fine balloon. It bobbed beautifully in the breeze, and followed Sheila on its string wherever she went.

Soon some children came by and called to Sheila. "What a marvellous balloon! Sheila, we are going for a walk in the woods. Do come. You can bring your balloon too."

"No, thank you. It's too hot," said Sheila. "I'm going to stay here in the garden and not go walking in the heat. I might get a sunstroke."

"Don't be silly," said the children. But Sheila wouldn't go with them, so they left her.

The little girl walked round the garden with her balloon blowing behind her. Suddenly the breeze blew extra hard – and the string slipped through Sheila's fingers! Up in the air at once went the balloon, quite free, and the string dangled down, blowing in the wind.

"Oh, oh, come back, balloon!" cried Sheila in dismay. But the balloon didn't come back, of course. It was glad to be free, and it flew joyfully over the hedge, bob-bob-bobbing as it went, blowing higher and higher like an enormous blue-and-yellow bubble.

"Mother, Mother, my balloon's gone!" shouted Sheila, rushing indoors.

"Go after it then, silly child!" said her mother. "Hurry, or you will lose it."

Sheila ran down the garden path and out of the gate. She ran down the lane, panting and puffing, for she was not used to running. The balloon bobbed ahead of her all the time.

It hopped over a hedge into a field. Sheila couldn't hop over the hedge because it was too high, so she had to run to the gate and climb over it. By the time she was in the field, the balloon was right at the other side! And it hopped over the hedge there!

"Oh dear, oh dear, I'll never catch you!" cried Sheila in despair. Across the field she ran, just in time to see the balloon disappear into the woods.

And when she got to the woods, there was no balloon to be seen! It had gone.

"Oh!" wept poor Sheila, "has it gone pop? I do wish I could see it. Well, I'll hunt and hunt for it till I find it!"

So she ran through the woods, looking for the balloon. She couldn't see it anywhere. And at last, tired out, she sat down under a tree.

*The balloon bobbed ahead all the time*

The woods were very still. Overhead were millions of green leaves, cool and shady. A bird suddenly sang a loud, sweet song.

"How lovely!" thought Sheila, lifting her hot face upwards. "I never heard a bird singing so sweetly before. I wonder what bird it is."

The bird flew down. It was a big thrush and the freckles showed beautifully on its breast. It seemed very tame and hopped quite near to Sheila. The little girl did not dare to move in case she frightened it away.

It threw two or three dead leaves over with its beak as if it were looking for something. Then it gave a cheerful call and flew back to the trees.

Almost at once a red squirrel came bounding down another tree, and looked at Sheila with the brightest black eyes she had ever seen. Then, to her great surprise and delight, it scampered right over to her and sniffed at her hands to see if she had any food for it.

"Oh, you darling, lovely thing!" whispered Sheila, not daring to talk loudly in case she frightened it away. "I love your big bushy tail. I love your bright eyes and dear little paws. Come nearer. Come on to my knee."

But the squirrel dashed away again and scampered up a tree, springing from one bough to the next in a really marvellous manner. Sheila thought he was wonderful.

Then a tiny mouse scampered by, its small black nose twitching, and its tail swinging behind it. It saw Sheila, stood for a moment to look at her, and then darted down a hole. And then a baby rabbit came out of a much bigger hole and sat up to wash itself.

It didn't seem to see the little girl at all. She kept perfectly still and watched. The rabbit first put down one ear and then another, and washed them both most carefully. Then it did a little hop, skip, and jump all about and darted off.

"It was just as if it was doing it all especially for me," said Sheila in delight. "I wonder what will come next."

Nothing came, and as Sheila sat there, her back against a tree, her eye caught sight of something glowing red not far off. She got up to see what it was.

"Wild red strawberries! Oh, how perfectly lovely!" cried Sheila, and she popped one into her mouth. It tasted so sweet and juicy. The little girl ate about twelve, and then she thought she would take some home to her mother.

So she gathered some, and put them into her handkerchief, wrapped carefully in a big leaf. She set out for home and forgot all about her balloon. She saw some tall yellow flowers growing by the path and stopped to pick a big bunch. "Mother will love these," thought Sheila. "I wonder what they are called. I wish I knew."

She hadn't gone very far before she heard the voices of the other children. When they saw Sheila they were most astonished.

"Sheila! Did you come for a walk after all? We thought you said you couldn't possibly."

"Well," said Sheila, going rather red, "well – I didn't exactly go for a walk. I went after my balloon. It flew away in the wind. I've been hunting for it everywhere."

"Did you find it?" asked the children. "You don't look very miserable, so you can't have lost it."

"I *have* lost it!" said Sheila. "But I found quite a lot of other things – these flowers and these strawberries – and I saw a red squirrel, and heard a thrush sing to me. And a mouse ran by and looked at me, and a rabbit, quite a baby one, come out of his hole and showed me how he washed his ears one by one. And then he did a sort of little dance for me."

"Well, we told you we had great fun on our walks, and you never seemed to believe us," said the other children. "Come on – it's time we went home."

So home they all went. And how pleased Sheila's mother was with her wild strawberries! She put them on to a little glass dish, and put the big yellow flowers into water.

"What a lovely walk you must have had!" she said. "Oh, Sheila, how funny – you will never, never go for a walk, but your balloon took you for one!"

"Yes – it took me – but it didn't bring me back," said Sheila sadly. "I've lost it."

"No, you haven't!" said her mother. "Look in your bedroom, Sheila! It came bobbing back into the garden when the wind changed! So I caught it for you and it's in your room!"

"Oh, now I *am* happy!" cried Sheila joyfully, and she ran up to get the balloon.

"You made me go for a long, long walk," said Sheila to her balloon. "Because of you I heard the thrush sing a song to me, and I saw the little animals of the wood, and found strawberries and flowers. And tomorrow, balloon, you and I are going for a walk again. What a lot I've missed, through being lazy!"

So now Sheila goes out with the other children, and knows just as much as they do about the hills and the woods and the streams. But wasn't it funny that her balloon had to teach her!

## Poor Dicky Duck

Dicky Duck was a lovely toy. He lived in Jane's nursery, and he had a long yellow beak, bright eyes, and he was dressed in a smart sailor suit.

All the toys loved him because he was so jolly and cheery. They liked his quack too. He always quacked if his tummy was pressed, and when he quacked, his beak opened and shut. Sometimes at night it was quite surprising that he didn't wake up the whole household because he quacked so much.

And then one morning poor Dicky Duck had a dreadful accident. Jane had been playing with him, and when it was time for her to go for her morning walk, she put Dicky Duck up on the bookshelf.

"Sit there, Dicky Duck," she said. "You can see all the nursery from there!"

Then off she went to put on her hat and coat, and soon the door banged, and there was silence in the house.

The clockwork mouse ran out of the toy-cupboard and began to chase his own tail, round and round on the hearth-rug. The dolls laughed to see him. The golliwog shouted to him:

"Hurry, mouse, hurry! You'll catch it if you run fast enough."

Dicky Duck had a fine view of the little mouse. He leaned over to see even better, and then he began to laugh. And he laughed so much that he fell right off the bookshelf!

Crash! He fell to the floor, and for a minute he lay there, hardly knowing what had happened to him. And when at last he sat up again, what a dreadful sight met his eyes! His lovely beak lay on the floor! It was broken right off.

Dicky Duck was so frightened that he just sat and stared. He did feel funny without a beak. He couldn't open it and quack, because there was no beak to open. He couldn't even quack.

All the toys came running round, staring in horror. "Your beak!" cried the golliwog, picking it up. "Your poor beak! Dicky Duck, whatever are you going to do?"

But Dicky couldn't answer. He sat and stared miserably at the toys, big tears coming into his eyes.

"You don't look like a duck any more," said the teddy-bear sadly. "I don't know what you look like. You look simply horrid."

Dicky Duck had no handkerchief, so he wiped his eyes on his sleeve. But still the tears came pouring out. How awful to be a duck and not look like one! How dreadful to look simply horrid!

"Can't we do something?" squeaked the clockwork mouse, running up, quite forgetting to chase his tail. "Oh, can't we do something – stick the beak on again – or sew it?"

"It can't be sewn on," said the bear, taking the beak into his paw. "But it might be stuck on. Where's the glue?"

They got the tube of glue from the nursery drawer, and squeezed some out on to the broken edge of the beak. They pressed the beak very hard on to the duck's head. It stuck there! How pleased all the toys were!

Dicky pressed his tummy hard, so that he could quack and say thank you. But as soon as he opened his beak to quack, it fell off on to the ground again. Wasn't it dreadful!

The toys stared in dismay. Then they picked it up, glued it again and stuck it back. "You'd better not quack for a while, Dicky," they said.

So Dicky Duck sat on the floor, quite still, waiting for his beak to stick tightly. He didn't at all like the smell of the glue. He thought it smelt of bad fish. But he couldn't quack to tell his friends that, in case his beak fell off again.

"It's stuck hard now," said the bear at last, trying to move it. "I'll press your tummy to make you quack, Dicky. I think your beak is all right now."

But, oh dear, as soon as Dicky opened his beak, it fell off again. It was just no use at all. Dicky began to cry again, and the bear made him get up after a minute or two because his tears made a puddle round him, and the bear said he would catch cold.

"And what you would do if you had a cold and no beak to sneeze with, I don't know," said the bear kindly.

The duck went into the toy-cupboard and sat right at the back, because he felt so ashamed without any beak at all. The toys went over by the fire and began to talk together quietly.

"I'm afraid Jane will hate Dicky Duck when she sees how awful he looks without any beak," said the sailor-doll.

"Do you think he will be thrown away?" asked the clockwork mouse anxiously.

The bear nodded sadly. "Yes," he said. "I'm afraid he will. I remember once that we had a wooden horse here, and when two of his legs broke off, he was thrown away at once. I'm afraid we shall have to say good-bye to dear old Dicky Duck soon if we can't think of something."

"It's a pity there are no fairies or pixies living anywhere near," said the golliwog gloomily. "We could get a bit of magic from them to help Dicky, perhaps."

"What's a fairy?" asked the clockwork mouse, who had never even seen one, he was so young and new.

"A fairy is a person with a frilly frock and a silver wand, and wings at her back, and she can do magic things," said the bear.

The clockwork mouse stared at him. "Well, I know where one lives," he said.

"You don't," said the golliwog.

"I do, I do," said the mouse. "There's a fairy living inside a box in the cupboard out in the hall. I peeped inside and saw her. She's sweet. She wears a frilly frock and a silver crown, and she has a silver stick in her hand, and wings at her back. She spoke to me, and asked me to let her out."

"You're telling stories, Mouse," said the toys in astonishment. "Fairies don't live in boxes, silly."

"Well, this one does," said the mouse. "Wait till to-night and I'll take you to see her."

The boys told Dicky Duck to stay hidden at the back of the cupboard so that Jane wouldn't see him. He had a very big pocket in his trousers, and they put his broken beak into that. They did hope that Jane wouldn't look for him.

She didn't. She didn't think of him at all, but played with her bricks till bedtime. And when the nursery was

90

dark, except for the glow of the fire, the toys crept out of the cupboard once more.

"Now, Mouse, show us where this hidden fairy is," said the bear. "Really and truly I think you are just making it all up."

The clockwork mouse led them out of the room and into the hall. He was a great one for running everywhere, and exploring everything, and there wasn't a cupboard or shelf he hadn't sniffed around by now. He nosed open the door of the cupboard. On the bottom shelf lay a lot of boxes. The golliwog lifted the lid of one.

"Oh! These are all the pretty ornaments off the Christmas tree we had last year!" he said in delight. "Look! And in this next box there are Christmas-tree candles. And in this one there is shiny tinsel. So *this* is where Jane's mummy put all the Christmas-tree things. I wondered where they had gone!"

"Now where's this fairy?" the bear asked the mouse.

"Here," said the mouse, trying to lift up the lid of a long narrow box with his sharp nose. "Help me to raise the lid, Bear, and you will see her. I really have been telling you the truth!"

The bear lifted up the lid – and all the toys looked inside the box. They stared and stared – for there, lying quite quietly, and looking very beautiful indeed, was the fairy doll who had been at the top of the Christmas tree!

"Oh! It's not a fairy. It's the fairy doll!" cried the golliwog in delight. "I always wondered what had happened to her, the dear, beautiful thing!"

"Oh – is she a doll?" said the mouse in disappoint-
91

ment. "I *really* thought she was a fairy. She's just like one, isn't she?"

The fairy doll stared up at all the toys out of bright blue eyes. Her golden hair lay round her head like a yellow mist. She had a little smile on her red lips.

"Hallo, Toys!" she said. "Oh, how lovely it is to speak to somebody! I am so terribly lonely lying here all day and all night, never speaking, never playing – with only the little clockwork mouse to peep at me sometimes."

"You poor lonely thing!" cried the kind-hearted bear. "We'll help you out! You shall come and play with us. You can easily creep back into your box at dawn, and we can put your lid on safely. Come along – stand up!"

The fairy-doll's legs were stiff with not being used, but she managed to stand up and get out of the box. Then, with the golliwog holding her up one side and the bear the other, she walked slowly across to the nursery. And in twenty minutes she was playing happily on the carpet with the toys. She showed them her pretty silver wings and her lovely wand. The mouse thought she was wonderful, and he ran to tell Dicky Duck about the new toy.

"Peep out and see her," he said. So the duck peeped out – and the fairy doll saw him. He looked so very, very peculiar without his beak that she gave a scream and ran away.

"What's that dreadful creature looking out of the cupboard?" she cried. The toys told her.

"It's only poor Dicky Duck. His beak is broken off, so he is very unhappy. We did try to stick it on, but it wouldn't stick. We thought maybe if you were a real fairy you could use magic and stick it on for him – but you are only a fairy doll," said the bear.

The doll stared at him and smiled. She tapped him with her silver wand. "Bear!" she said. "I may be only a fairy *doll* – but I'll tell you a lovely secret. There is always a little magic in a fairy-doll's wand – and I'll use it for your Dicky Duck, if you like. I've been saving the bit of magic up for something really important – and I think this is important, don't you?"

"Very important!" shouted all the toys, and they ran to get Dicky Duck. He took his broken beak out of his trousers' pocket and held it out to the doll. She neatly pressed it to his head, and then tapped all round it with her wand, chanting the only magic words she knew:

"Abra-cadabra, abra-cadabra!"

And hey presto, his beak was on! You couldn't even see the crack where it had broken off! It was really marvellous. Dicky Duck was so delighted that he put his wing round the fairy doll and gave her a fine kiss with his mended beak. He pressed his tummy and his beak opened at once and he began to quack.

"Quack, quack, quack, quack!" he said. "Quack, quack, quack, quack, quack!"

The fairy doll laughed to see and hear him quacking. "You look lovely," she said. "And I do like your voice."

There was no more magic in her wand. She had used it all up. But she didn't mind, because now every night she could play with the toys! And you may be sure that Dicky Duck sees her back safely to her cupboard, and carefully puts on her lid for her. It's so much nicer for her to come out and play than to lie still in a box all the year round!

There was once a tiresome little boy called William. He was the sort of person who is always making trouble and interfering with other people.

He took Ann's bricks away when she began to play with them. He knocked down John's dominoes just when he had built a nice little house with them. He took Jane's plasticine man and squeezed him so that he wasn't a dear little red man any longer but just a nasty mess.

But wasn't he cross when anyone was unkind to him! Didn't he make a fuss if anyone tore a book of his or upset his castle of bricks!

He was tiresome to his mother and his teacher too. He wouldn't do as he was told. He wouldn't run an errand, he wouldn't stay behind at school and tidy the room properly – he just wouldn't do anything he didn't want to!

"My goodness!" he would say, "why should I run down to the grocer's just when I want to read my book!"

"Just to be kind, William," said his mother.

"My goodness, *I* don't want to be kind!" William would say. "Being kind is a perfect nuisance. It means doing things you don't want to all the time. My goodness, I shan't be as silly as that!"

"I can't imagine why you are always saying 'My

94

goodness!'" said his mother crossly. "You haven't any goodness or kindness at all!"

William stamped out of the room. "My goodness!" he said to himself, "My goodness, people are always grumbling at me! I've a good mind to run away, then they'll be sorry!"

He stopped and thought about it for a while, and then he stole back indoors, took his school satchel, put into it some chocolate from his drawer, some biscuits from the biscuit-jar, some apples and bananas from the fruit-dish, and some nuts from the nut-bowl. Then he put a scarf round his neck and crept out of the house by the side-door.

"My goodness, what a shock everyone will get when they find I'm gone!" said William to himself. "They'll be sorry then that they grumbled and scolded so, and tried to make me do things for them all day long!"

He ran down to the bottom of the garden and let himself out by the gate there. A lane ran at the end of his garden. William went down it. The lane led to a small cottage and stopped there. But a little path ran round the cottage into a thick wood. William didn't often go into the wood because the trees were thick and the wood was dark. People had often been lost in the wood, it was so very large, and the trees were so very close together.

"Nobody would think of looking for me in the wood," thought William. "I'd be quite hidden there. I shall find a hollow tree or something and make it my home today. I've plenty of food to eat. What a shock everyone will get when they find me gone! My goodness, this is a fine idea of mine!"

He went into the wood. It really was very dark, but
95

William wasn't a bit afraid. He was a tiresome boy, but certainly not a coward. He quite enjoyed pushing his way into the wood, through the bushes and trees. He soon lost the path, and after that he just went where the way was easiest.

Presently he came to a lovely little glade where primroses grew by the hundred, and green moss shone brightly. A tiny stream ran through the glade and made a bubbling noise. William sat down near it and took out some biscuits and chocolate.

"My goodness, I'm hungry!" he said out loud. A blackbird hopped down beside him in a most friendly way. Then a robin fluttered down and stood on the moss nearby, making a little creamy noise in his throat.

Did William give them a crumb? No, of course not! He scrabbled in the moss and found some small pebbles – and he threw them at the two surprised birds! They flew off at once, their bright eyes full of anger.

William finished his biscuits and chocolate. He threw the paper away on the moss instead of putting it into his bag to take home. Then he took a stick and began to dig up the moss, just for fun. Soon he had little bits littered all over the place. Then he pulled the heads off about twenty primroses and threw them into the stream to see them float away.

William was just about to pull a few more when he had a great surprise. A door flew open in a nearby tree, and a red-faced gnome looked out. William knew it was a gnome because he had seen pictures of one in a book. He stared at the little man in surprise.

"My goodness!" he said, "you gave me a shock, popping out like that!"

"And what sort of a shock do you think you have

96

given *me*!" shouted the gnome, jumping out of his tree. "Look at my lovely moss pulled up – and my primroses spoilt – and that nasty bit of paper flying about – and how *dare* you throw stones at my blackbird and robin!"

"My goodness!" said William. "What a temper you're in!"

The gnome was very small, but as soon as he had jumped from the tree, he grew as large as William. This was a great surprise, and the boy stared in astonishment.

"My goodness!" he said, as usual.

"That's the third time you've talked about your goodness!" said the gnome scornfully. "Where is it, I should like to know?"

"Where is what?" asked William, puzzled.

"Your goodness!" said the gnome. "Have you got any goodness at all? Aren't you the boy that never does anything for anyone? Aren't you the tiresome boy called William?"

"You *are* rude!" said William crossly. "My goodness, you are –"

"There you go again! Your goodness!" cried the gnome in a rage. "Why do you keep talking about your goodness when you haven't got any at all?"

"Now you just be quiet," said William angrily, getting up. "I'll tell my mother about you when I get home, and she will come into this wood with a great big stick."

The gnome laughed, and made himself twice as big as William at once. He seemed to be able to go large or small just as he liked. William was rather frightened when he saw the gnome towering over him, larger than a grown-up.

"Now just you listen to me, you tiresome, nasty little boy," said the gnome in a rather loud voice. "You won't get out of this wood till you find your goodness! See? Now you go and find your goodness and bring it back to me, and I'll show you the way out of the wood. Not till then will you leave here! Ho, ho – what a job you'll have finding your goodness!"

"Don't be so silly," said William at once. "As if I'd go looking for my goodness. You can't find goodness! I shall leave this wood at once, and go home and tell my mother what a nasty person lives in this wood. I wouldn't be surprised if my mother orders your tree to be chopped down!"

The gnome laughed again. It wasn't a very pleasant sound, and as William was really a bit afraid that the gnome might grow even larger all of a sudden, he made up his mind to go back home at once. It wasn't such fun to run away after all if he met people like this gnome, who was so rude to him.

"My goodness!" he said, as he turned to go. "What an unpleasant person you are!"

William made his way between the trees, trying to find the path home. But after a little while he knew that it wasn't any good. He seemed to be getting deeper and deeper into the wood instead of nearer home. This wasn't nice at all!

He stopped and shouted loudly, "Hie! Hie! Is anyone about?"

Nobody answered at first. Then a brownie peeped from behind a tree. "I'm here," he said. "What do you want?"

"I want my way home," said William. "Out of this horrid wood."

"It isn't a horrid wood," said the brownie. "It's a lovely wood. You should see it in the autumn when the trees are all red, yellow, and brown!"

"I don't want to see it in the autumn or the spring or the winter," said William rudely. "I want to get out of it and never come back."

"Well, maybe I'll tell you the way if you will do something for me," said the brownie. "Look, do you see this baby bird I'm holding? It fell out of the nest up in this tree, and I want to put it back. But I'm not tall enough to haul myself up from that branch there. *You* could easily climb up, then I could hand you the baby bird."

"No, thank you," said William. "I don't like touching birds. And if it's silly enough to fall out of the nest, well, let it!"

"You horrid boy!" said the brownie in astonishment. "I shouldn't have thought there could possibly be anyone in the world who wouldn't help a baby thing like this!"

"My goodness! This wood seems to be full of nothing but rude people who grumble at me!" said William crossly. "Tell me the way out."

"Find it yourself," said the brownie, and popped back behind the tree. William didn't see him again. The boy turned round and went another way, pushing through the thick trees and bushes.

"It wouldn't be a bad idea if I climbed a tree to the top, and tried to see which way I should go," thought William. So he chose a tree that seemed easy enough to climb, and up he went. But the tree was not as tall as the others around it, so all the boy could see was the top of other trees!

He climbed down again – but before he reached the bottom branches, a bough cracked beneath his foot. It broke off – and William was suddenly standing on nothing! He clutched at a nearby branch and missed it. Down he fell and down.

Crash! He landed in a bush below – but, oh my, it was a bramble bush, thick and overgrown. The prickles caught hold of poor William and scratched his hands, legs, and face. He couldn't get out. He was stuck!

"My goodness!" said William. "Whatever am I to do?"

William wriggled in the blackberry bush, trying his hardest to get out. The more he wriggled, the more the prickles scratched him. It was horrid.

His hands and legs were bleeding with the scratches, and his clothes were torn. He felt very much as if he would like to cry, but he knew he was too old to do that. So he blinked away something that felt like tears, and shouted at the top of his voice:

"Help! Help!"

At once a plump little old woman came up, her green eyes twinkling kindly. "My poor boy!" she said. "Let me help you out!"

In a trice she was helping William, and he was soon standing on the grass again. The old woman led him between the trees to a tiny cottage in a clearing.

"I'll bathe your scratches and mend your clothes," she said. So William stood in a tiny kitchen, and the green-eyed old dame gently bathed his horrid scratches and bound up one very nasty one. Then, with a needle and thread that must surely have been magic, she mended every hole in his clothes.

"Thank you," said William gratefully. It was nice to meet someone gentle and kind, when he was in trouble. "Do you think you could tell me the way out of this wood? A horrid gnome told me I wouldn't get out till I'd found some goodness – which is really silly, of course."

"Oh – the gnome told you that, did he?" said the old woman. "Well, if he said that, he's right, little boy. You'll have to find some somehow!"

"Oh, dear!" said William in dismay. "I wish I'd never come into this silly wood." He looked at the kind old woman, and spoke rather shyly.

"Please – you are awfully good and kind – could you give me a bit of *your* goodness, then I could get out of this wood!"

"Well – I wouldn't know how to give you any of mine," said the old woman. "But look – go to the Toadstool Pixie and ask her if she can give you any of hers. She has the kindest heart, and is always helping people. I'll show you where she lives. I've got to take a parcel to a friend of mine who lives near her."

William set off with the green-eyed old dame. She was almost bent double under a heavy parcel.

"I'm not so young as I was," she said. "I'm afraid I must walk slowly with this heavy load."

William felt sorry. "Let me carry it for you," he said. "I'm strong, really I am. You've been so kind to me, I'd like to take your parcel."

"Oh, thank you," said the old woman, and she gave William the parcel. It was dreadfully heavy. William had never carried a parcel for anyone in his life, but although it was heavy, he didn't mind at all. It was rather a nice feeling to be helping such a kind old lady.

He staggered along, and at last they came to a very large toadstool. There was a narrow door in the stalk,

101

and the old woman rapped on it. It flew open and a bright-eyed pixie looked out.

"This boy wants a bit of help," said the old woman. "Just see to him, will you, Toadstool Pixie? I'm going on to a friend of mine. Good-bye, little boy. I hope you find what you want."

The pixie looked at William. "What do you want?" she asked kindly. "I'll help you in any way I can, you may be sure."

"Well – do you think you could give me a bit of your goodness?" asked William. "The gnome in this wood said I wouldn't be able to get out unless I found some goodness."

"Did he really?" said the Toadstool Pixie, puzzled. "Well, I don't know how to give goodness away, or I would certainly give you some. Come indoors and let me make you some cocoa. You look hungry! I'll give you some biscuits too."

She took William into her toadstool house. Inside the door there was a tiny spiral staircase that went winding round to the large top of the toadstool. William found himself much too big, finally, but he enjoyed squeezing up the stairs and into the funny-shaped room at the top.

The pixie set a kettle on a tiny stove to boil. Then she went to a biscuit-tin – but when she opened it, she cried out in dismay.

"Oh! Someone has been here and taken all my biscuits! Oh, it's too bad. Little boy, I'm very sorry, but there isn't a cake or a biscuit I can give you. Do forgive me!"

The pixie's eyes filled with tears. She was the kindest little thing, and it seemed dreadful to her not to be able to offer William even a biscuit.

William did feel sorry for her. He patted her on the back, and wiped her eyes with his rather dirty handkerchief. Then he suddenly had a fine idea.

"I've got some fruit in my satchel!" he said. "Let's have that instead!"

So he got out the bananas, apples, and nuts, and the two of them sat in the toadstool house, and ate them with the hot cocoa. It was great fun, and William loved it.

"You're a kind fellow," said the Toadstool Pixie. "You really are."

It was the first time that anyone had ever called William kind. It was most surprising how much he liked it. He had always thought it would be such a nuisance to be a kind person, always having to do things for other people – but, dear me, it wasn't bad after all! In fact, it was really good to see someone smiling happily into his eyes and calling him a kind fellow.

"Well, I must be going," said William, when the fruit was finished. "I suppose you couldn't possibly tell me where I could get a bit of goodness? I've a feeling I shan't get out of this wood till I find some."

"You might try the Friendly Goblin who lives just round the corner," said the Toadstool Pixie. "He is such a friendly fellow. He might help you somehow. He knows a bit of magic, and perhaps he could give you a bit of his goodness for your own."

William went down the tiny winding staircase and called good-bye as he made his way round the trees to where the pixie had pointed. He came to a fat oak tree,

*William went down the tiny staircase*

and in it, as the pixie had said, he found a round door. He knocked on it.

"Come in!" cried a voice. So William opened the door and climbed in, though it was a bit of a squeeze. Inside the tree there was a perfectly round room, very cosy and very small. A tiny goblin sat on a stool, mending a pair of boots. He turned a pair of friendly green eyes on William.

"Hallo, sonny!" he said. "Anything I can do for you?"

"Well, there *is* something, if only you could manage it," said William. "I've been told that I can't get out of this wood unless I find some goodness somewhere. But I can't seem to get any. The Toadstool Pixie says you know a bit of magic and might help me."

The Friendly Goblin looked over the tops of his glasses at William. He shook his head.

"I'm sorry," he said. "I'd help you if I could – but goodness isn't a thing that one person can give to another, like sweets or presents! You only find goodness in one place, and that's deep down in a person's heart. I can't get at my goodness to give any to you. You can only grow goodness in your own heart, you see."

"Oh," said William, most disappointed. "Can you tell when people have got their goodness all right or not? I mean, the gnome in this wood told me that I must go and find my goodness, because I hadn't any. How did he know I hadn't?"

"Maybe he looked into your eyes," said the goblin. "That's the best way to tell. Kind eyes, merry eyes, happy eyes, smiling eyes – you can almost see the goodness behind them, you know. Maybe you behaved badly to him too. I don't know. Anyway, you can always tell."

The little fellow smiled up at William, and then turned to mend his boot again. He took a knife to cut a piece of leather, and as he cut it, the knife slipped and cut his hand very badly. He gave a cry and dropped both boot and knife.

"Oh, I say!" cried William, in dismay. "What a horrid thing to happen. Look – here's my hanky – rather dirty, I'm afraid, but do use it to mop up your hand. Can I get a bandage? Does it hurt?"

The goblin mopped up his hand and then went to a bowl of water. He bathed the cut, found a piece of clean linen, and then William neatly bound up his hand for him.

"You're a good friend," said the goblin, patting William's arm. "I'm really very grateful to you."

William beamed. "Don't mention it," he said, but all the same he was glad that the Friendly Goblin *had* mentioned it.

"I suppose you couldn't possibly tell me the way out of the wood, could you?" asked William.

"No. If the gnome says you can't go out until you've found your goodness, you'll have to stay, I'm afraid," said the goblin. "But if I were you I would go back to him and say you're sorry."

The Friendly Goblin took him outside his tree and told him the way to go. William said good-bye and ran off.

It wasn't long before he came to the gnome's tree again. He knocked on the door. It opened, and the red-faced gnome, now gone small again, looked out.

"Hallo," he said. "You back again?"

"Yes," said William. "I really have tried to find a bit of goodness, Gnome, but nobody can give me any at

106

all. I'm sorry I spoilt your moss and your primroses, and frightened your birds. Please let me go out of this wood and get back home."

"So you couldn't find your goodness?" said the gnome, and he came right out of his tree. He looked into William's eyes.

"Now here's a funny thing!" he said. "A very funny thing! You *have* found your goodness! I can see it in your eyes, so I know there is some in your heart. Now where did you find it, I wonder?"

"I simply can't imagine," said William, in surprise.

"Let me look again," said the gnome. "Ah – did you help an old woman? Yes – you did! Were you kind to the Friendly Goblin? Yes – you were!"

"My goodness!" said William, in delight. "Can you see all that? My goodness me!"

"Yes – you can say 'My goodness' all you like now," said the gnome, smiling. "You've got some – and a very good thing too! Keep it, my boy, keep it – it's one of the things that really matters! Good-bye! Keep straight along that path and you'll soon be home!"

William was simply delighted. He set off running down the path and was soon out of the wood and in the lane that led to his garden.

And the curious thing was that although it seemed to William as if he had been away a long time, nobody had missed him at all!

But they did notice something – he had got a little of the goodness he was always exclaiming about! Do *you* ever say "My goodness!" Well, if you do, I hope you have some!

## The Doll on the Christmas Tree

Raggy was a funny little doll. She was called Raggy because she was stuffed with rags, and was very soft and cuddly. But she was old now, and her face looked queer. She had odd eyes, her hair was made of yellow wool, her nose was flat, and her teeth and lips were made of white and red stitches.

Every Christmas the children sorted out their old toys, and put aside those that they could spare. They were given away to children who had very few toys. But Raggy was never given away because the children loved her so much.

That Christmas a great many new toys came to the nursery. There were three children there, and they all had aunts and uncles who gave them lovely toys. So a new railway train came, a new clockwork motor-car, three new dolls, a doll's house, a beautiful golliwog and a blue teddy bear.

The old toys looked at the new ones, and thought how clean and shining and beautiful they were. The new toys looked at the old ones, and turned up their noses at them.

"What a dirty creature you are!" said the new blue bear to the old brown one.

"What a battered creature you are!" said the new golly to the old one.

Then all the new toys stared at Raggy.

"Are you a doll or a bit of rubbish?" asked the new curly-haired doll.

"Why don't you wash your dirty old clothes?" asked the doll with the red hair-ribbon.

"I hope we haven't got to live in the same toy cupboard as *you*," said the new sailor doll. "You smell horrid – old and dirty!"

Raggy felt sad. She *was* old and she *was* dirty. She couldn't wash her clothes because they were sewn on to her, and she couldn't get them off. She sometimes tried to brush her yellow hair, but it is difficult to brush wool and make it look neat. Usually brushing her woollen hair made it very fuzzy indeed.

"I'm sorry I look so old and dirty," said Raggy. "I hope you will be happy in this nursery. The three children are very kind."

"We should be happy if we didn't have to live with people like you, and the dirty old teddy and the battered old golly," said the curly-haired doll unkindly.

"Now stop talking like that," said big Jumbo from his corner. "We have lived here for years, and the nursery is ours. You are newcomers. Behave yourselves."

"The idea! Talking to us like that!" said the blue bear. "I've a good mind to take that elephant by his tail and pull him out of the nursery! He should live in the boxroom, not here. He's quite out-of-date!"

Jumbo was so angry that he ran at the bear and nearly knocked him over. The bear skipped neatly out of the way. "That elephant has no manners at all!" growled the bear. "What sort of a nursery is this that we've come into?"

Now the three children were giving a party after Christmas to all their little friends. They wrote out the invitations and posted them. They dressed the big Christmas tree in the hall, and covered it with shining

109

ornaments and candles, and long gleaming strips of tin-foil that shone like icicles.

Then they tied gay little presents on the tree for their guests. It looked simply lovely.

But when they went to buy a fairy doll for the tree, they couldn't get one anywhere!

"Sorry, miss, but we have none this year," all the shops said. The children were bitterly disappointed. They talked about it in the nursery, and all the toys listened.

"We *must* have a fairy doll at the top of the tree," said Hilda. "It doesn't look right unless we do."

"A fairy doll is magic, and she can do magic with her wand," said Ken. "Everyone knows that."

"I wonder if we'd better put one of our new toys at the top of the tree instead?" said Polly.

All the new toys pricked up their ears at that. My goodness – to be at the top of the Christmas tree would be a very fine thing!

"I should look sweet there," said the curly-haired doll.

"I am just about the right size," said the doll with the red hair-ribbon.

"A sailor doll at the top of the tree would be marvel-lous," said the sailor doll.

"I'm sure all the children would rather have *me* than you," said the golliwog, proudly.

"They would shout with delight if *I* was there!" said the blue bear.

Raggy listened to them all and sighed. It would be marvellous to be at the top of the Christmas tree, watching the lighted candles shine, and the ornaments glitter. "But I must be glad that I wasn't put in the dustbin this year," thought the little raggy-doll. "After all, I *am* very old and very dirty!"

Now the children's mother was sorry because her three children were so disappointed about the fairy doll. She wondered what she could do about it. One night, when they were in bed, she went into the nursery and looked into the toy cupboard. All the new toys were thrilled. They felt sure she had come to choose one of them to put at the top of the tree.

So she had – but she didn't somehow think that any of the toys in the cupboard were quite right for the tree.

Raggy wasn't in the cupboard. The curly-haired doll had turned her out that night. "We are not going to let you share the cupboard with us," she said. "You are so ugly and old and dirty. You ought to be in the dust-bin."

Raggy had gone to a corner and curled up there, very miserable. It was bad enough to be old and dirty, without being told so a dozen times a day.

Mother shut the cupboard door, and then she suddenly saw Raggy curled up in the corner. She picked her up and looked at her.

"Dear little doll!" she said. "Hilda had you when she was a baby, and all the children have loved you, little Raggy."

She carried Raggy out of the nursery with her. She went to her work-room, and there she set to work on the old doll. She unpicked her dirty clothes, and there lay Raggy on the table without any clothes at all, feeling rather cold and queer.

"You are going to be a beautiful fairy doll, old Raggy!" said Mother. "I am going to make you a dress

111

of finest gauze, with frilly skirts, and little silver beads all over it! I shall make you shining silver wings, and give you a beautiful wand to wave. I shall wash your yellow woollen hair and make it shine like gold. I shall give you a silver crown to wear! How pleased the children will be!"

Mother worked hard all the evening. She made Raggy a lovely frilly dress sewn with tiny silver beads. She made her a most beautiful pair of silver wings that stuck out behind Raggy like real ones. She washed Raggy's woollen hair and dried it, and it looked clean and golden. She made a silver crown and a silver wand, and she even made a little pair of silver shoes!

"There! You look lovely!" said Mother. "The prettiest fairy doll we have ever had, Raggy! I'll put you at the top of the tree!"

The next morning the children shouted in delight to see a fairy doll on the tree. "Mother! You got one after all! Oh, Mother, she's beautiful!"

Many children came to the party. They stared at the lovely fairy doll, and how they all longed to have her for their own! They talked about her as they sat at tea in the nursery.

"She's simply wonderful," they said. "She ought to be queen of your nursery, Hilda. She's the finest fairy doll we've ever seen. And she has such a sweet look on her face too – so kind and loving!"

The toys listened to all this. That night, when the children had gone, they talked together. "Let us go and see this beautiful fairy doll. Perhaps she would come and live here with us and be our queen. We haven't a queen. It would be a great thing if we could have a

*"There, you look lovely," said mother*

fairy doll for a queen, because then she could use the magic in her wand for us!"

So they all crept down into the hall to see the tree. The candles were no longer lighted. The tree stood there in the moonlight, its ornaments shining and its fairy doll looking mysterious and beautiful at the top.

"Look at her wings!" whispered the blue bear.

"Look at her wand!" said the curly-haired doll.

"It's a pity that ugly old Raggy isn't here to see her," said Jumbo. "I can't think where she has disappeared to. I hope she hasn't been put into the dustbin."

"Best place for her!" said the sailor doll. "My goodness me – how I love that fairy doll! I wish she would marry me and work some magic for me!"

Jumbo spoke humbly to the fairy doll. "Beautiful fairy doll, will you come and be our queen? We would be very proud of you."

"Thank you," said the fairy doll, in a voice that sounded rather familiar. "But are you quite sure you want me?"

"Of course!" said everyone. "Come down now and we will give a party for you, fairy doll!"

So the fairy doll climbed down from the tree and went with the toys to the nursery. Raggy didn't know that the toys thought she was a really-truly fairy doll. She thought they knew she was only Raggy dressed up. She smiled round at everyone, as happy as could be, and the toys loved her.

What a fuss they made of her! They told her dozens of times how beautiful she was. Raggy had never had such a wonderful time in her life!

And then the curly-haired doll said: "It's a pity that

114

dirty old Raggy isn't here, fairy doll! Perhaps you could have waved your wand over her and made her a bit cleaner and prettier. She *was* such an ugly creature!"

The fairy doll looked at the curly-haired doll, and then she spoke in her soft little voice.

"Don't you know that *I* am Raggy? It is true that I am a fairy doll now, too – but I am Raggy as well!"

All the toys stared in the greatest amazement – and then they saw that it was indeed Raggy – but what a different Raggy!

"Oh, Raggy – you haven't been put in the dustbin after all!" cried Jumbo, joyfully. "Dear little Raggy – you deserve to be queen, you deserve to be a fairy doll, because you have always been so good and kind. Your Majesty, I am delighted to see you again!"

All the old toys crowded round Raggy and fussed her. The new ones felt most awkward – dear me, suppose Raggy had magic in her wand and could punish them for their unkindness now! They thought they had better be nice to her too.

But Raggy knew what they were thinking. "I won't be your queen if you don't want me to be," she said. "I'll just be queen of the old toys. And don't think that I shall use the magic in my wand to punish you. I shall only use it to make you happy."

"Oh," said the curly-haired doll, staring at Raggy in surprise. "Oh! You *are* kind and good and forgiving. You deserve to be queen, you really do!"

"She does," said the sailor doll.

"She's a darling!" said the blue bear. And all the new toys curtsied and bowed to Raggy most politely and gracefully.

115

She is still queen of the nursery, and each Christmas she goes back to the top of the Christmas tree. I expect you'd like to see her there, wouldn't you? Well, if you get to know Hilda, Ken and Polly, just ask them to show you old Raggy. They will be delighted to!

## Which Would You Do?

Peter and Andy were playing catch with a cricket ball in Andy's garden. Mother knocked on the window.

"Don't play catch with your cricket ball in the garden!" she called. "You may break a window. Go into the field."

"Bother!" said Andy. "I don't want to go into the field. Peter, let's come down to the bottom of the garden and play there. My mother won't see us then."

Peter didn't like doing that. He thought they ought to go to the field. But Andy laughed at him.

"Oh, come on!" he said. "Are you afraid of getting into trouble? We shan't do any harm down there – so long as we don't let our ball go over the fence into old Surly's garden."

"All right," said Peter, and he made up his mind to be very careful. But Andy wasn't so careful, and after two or three wild throws, he made such a silly one that the ball flew up into the air – and over into Mr. Surly's garden. Then there was a crash of breaking glass!

The boys looked at one another in fright. "We've broken a pane in Mr. Surly's greenhouse," said Andy, in a low voice. "Come on – run to the house, quick!"

"But oughtn't we to go and tell him?" said Peter, as they ran to the house.

"Don't be silly! Do you want a scolding from Mr. Surly – do you want him to go round and tell your mother – and have to take all the money out of your money-box to pay for the pane of glass?" panted Andy.

"Well, it was really your fault," said Peter. "You threw that ball. I didn't."

"Oh– you would like to put all the blame on to me, and let *me* have the punishment, I suppose?" said Andy.

"No, I wouldn't," said Peter, at once. "I know I was as much to blame as you, Andy – I shouldn't have gone down there to play. We should both have gone to the field as your mother said."

Peter didn't stay to play with Andy after that. He went home. On the way he passed the bottom of Mr. Surly's garden. He peeped through a hole in the fence. He saw that two panes of glass were broken in the greenhouse, not one. No one was about. It seemed as if Mr. Surly hadn't heard the crash.

"There are tomato plants in that greenhouse," thought Peter. "I hope Mr. Surly knows the panes are broken – for if it happens to be frosty tonight, the frost may get in at those broken panes and spoil all his tomatoes. He's a greengrocer, so it would be a big loss to him."

The little boy went home, feeling very uncomfortable. How silly of Andy not to do as his mother said! How stupid of him to throw the ball so wildly!

"And how stupid of me not to be strong enough to say I would go to the field, and make him come with me," thought Peter. "It should be just as easy for me to

117

make Andy do right, as it is for Andy to make me do wrong."

Peter wondered if he could ask his mother what she thought, but he decided he must try and do it without giving Andy away.

"Mother," he said, "Is it a very mean thing to break something and then not tell the person?"

"Well, Peter, fancy asking me that!" said his mother. "No decent person would do a mean thing like that. It would mean they were too cowardly to own up. I am very glad to think I have a boy like you, with plenty of honesty and courage, who would always own up to anything."

That made Peter feel more uncomfortable than ever. He didn't know what to do. After all, *he* hadn't broken the pane! Still, it was just luck that he hadn't. It might quite well have been he who threw the ball over the fence.

"Mother, I'm just going out for a little while," said Peter, suddenly. His mother nodded. Peter got up and went out.

"I'm going to old Mr. Surly's – and I'm going to tell him that the glass got broken with my ball," he said to himself. "I need not say it was Andy who threw the ball and broke it. I can take the blame for both of us, without giving Andy away. I mustn't tell tales, I know – but, on the other hand, I can't let Mr. Surly go to bed tonight not knowing that the frost may get at his tomatoes.

Peter went to Mr. Surly's house. He knocked at the door. His knees felt a bit shaky, for it was well known that Mr. Surly disliked boys, ever since one had stolen a box of oranges from his backyard.

Mr. Surly came to the door. He had big, shaggy eyebrows that were very frightening. "What do you want?" he asked, sharply.

"Mr. Surly – I'm very sorry – but – you see, Mr. Surly – I was –" began Peter.

"Speak up, lad, speak up," said Mr. Surly.

"Well, Mr. Surly – it was like this. I was playing with my ball this afternoon – and it went over the fence – and it broke two panes of your greenhouse," said Peter, bringing it all out in a rush. "But if you will give me time to pay, I have a birthday next week, and I'm sure to get some money and I could bring it to you then!"

Mr. Surly looked at Peter from under his shaggy eyebrows. Then he said a surprising thing.

"I know all about the broken panes," he said. "I'm just mending them. I can't afford to let the frost get into my greenhouse."

"Oh!" said Peter.

"And I know this," said Mr. Surly, his shaggy eyebrows rising up, "I know this – you're not the boy that broke the panes!"

"Oh," said Peter again. He couldn't think of anything else to say.

"No," said Mr. Surly, "it was another boy who threw that ball and broke my panes. You were playing with him. But it wasn't you that broke the glass."

"Were you watching us then?" asked Peter.

"I just happened to be looking out of my bedroom window," said Mr. Surly. "And I saw you both. Now, my boy – you tell me this, please – why did you come and own up to something you didn't do?"

"Well – I didn't want you to lose all your tomatoes," said Peter, "and I couldn't very well tell tales on the other boy – and it *was* partly my fault, because I knew
119

we oughtn't to play there – and I'm not a coward, so I came to tell you."

"You're not a coward, though your knees are a bit shaky, aren't they?" said Mr. Surly, with an unexpected smile. "I like you. You're a fine boy, I think. You're one of the only boys I've ever met who gave a thought to other people – you actually thought of me losing my tomatoes! Ah, I've no time for the boys I see about now – rude, ill-mannered little things – always throwing stones and breaking things! Come in. I've got something for you."

Peter went in. The back of Mr. Surly's house opened into a yard, partly covered by a wooden roof. Here were stored sacks and barrels of all kinds. Mr. Surly went to a big barrel, knocked off the top and removed some straw.

A delicious smell came from the barrel. It was full of red-skinned apples, the last of the winter store.

"Now, you look here," said Mr. Surly, "see those apples? Well, there's one every day for you, if you like to come and get it. I always say a dishonest, untruthful child should be punished – and now I say that an honest, decent boy should be rewarded. You come every day and help yourself to one."

"Oh, thank you," said Peter, beaming. He loved apples, and got very few. "I shall only take one each day. You can trust me."

"Trust you! I know that!" said Mr. Surly. "People who can be trusted are the best on earth, man, woman, or boy or girl! And it's a pity we don't teach that more often in our schools, I say. You must have a very fine mother, who teaches you the right thing. I daresay your mother is proud of you – but just you be proud of your

*"There's an apple every day for you," said the man*

mother, too! It isn't many mothers can bring up a boy so well that he comes to own up to something he really ought not to be blamed for, in order to save someone's tomatoes."

"I *am* proud of my mother," said Peter. "And I shall give her one of my apples every other day."

"Nice boy," said Mr. Surly, and he gave Peter a clap on the back. "Nice boy! Come and see me whenever you like."

Peter went home with a ripe, juicy apple. He was going to give the very first one to his mother. He thought very hard as he went home, about all that Mr. Surly said. He *was* lucky to have a mother who told him the right things. He knew that.

He met Andy as he went home. Andy's eyes opened wide when he saw the lovely apple. "Wherever did you get that?" he said.

"From old Mr. Surly," said Peter. "And I'm to go and take one from the barrel every single day!"

"Why?" asked Andy, in the greatest astonishment.

"I'll tell you. It's very surprising," said Peter. "You see, I got worried about old Mr. Surly's tomatoes when I got home – and after a bit I saw it would be cowardly not to go and warn him about the broken panes, in case the frost got in tonight. So I went and warned him – and he was very pleased and said I could have an apple a day."

"You horrid thing – did you tell him *I* broke the panes?" cried Andy, fiercely.

"Of course not," said Peter. "How could you think I would tell tales like that? I just told him it was my ball that broke it, but I didn't say it was you who threw it. I tell you, I expected him to box my ears, and tell my mother, and be as surly as his name – but he wasn't."

Peter ran home. Andy stood staring after him. "I don't see why *I* shouldn't get apples, too," he thought. "I'll go and own up as well. Then old Mr. Surly will give me apples and say what a nice boy I am!"

But he didn't. He glared at Andy.

"Why didn't you come and own up when the other boy did?" he shouted. "Nasty little coward! You only came because you knew I gave him apples! Run away now, and mind this – if I meet your mother I'll tell her what kind of a son she's got."

Andy rushed away, upset and ashamed. I don't feel a bit sorry for him, do you? I think both boys deserved what they got!

# DRAGON BOOKS

The Dragon series is one of the finest Children's Libraries in print today. Enid Blyton, Lewis Carroll, Lady Antonia Fraser, Noel Streatfeild, Christine Pullein-Thompson, Mary O'Hara, show-jumper Pat Smythe and many others are all here to delight every child, whatever the mood or time of day. The Dragon authors represent a charming array of the most creative and time-honoured talents ever at work in the children's field – a pasture of absorbing and intimate pleasure through which wind our chequered Pied Pipers with their ageless tunes and tales, to the joy of millions of Dragon readers. As for Kid's Power – Dragon Books are just the thing to occupy young people finding out perhaps for the first time that peace and quiet can be lovely with a book, and who are beginning to discover for themselves the surprising fun in store for them in the world beyond the family.

If you or your parents have trouble in obtaining titles, please remember that they are available from Cash Sales Dept., P.O. Box 11, Falmouth, Cornwall, at the price shown plus 7p postage.

## ENID BLYTON

Summer Term at St Clare's  20p
The Twins at St Clare's  20p
Claudine at St Clare's  20p
Second Form at St Clare's  20p
Fifth Formers of St Clare's  20p

Mystery of the Banshee Towers  20p
Mystery of the Hidden House  20p
Mystery of Tally-Ho Cottage  20p
Mystery of the Missing Man  20p
Mystery of the Strange Messages  20p
Mystery of the Missing Necklace  20p
Mystery of the Burnt Cottage  20p
Mystery of the Pantomime Cat  20p

The O'Sullivan Twins  20p
Bimbo and Topsy  20p
Naughty Amelia Jane  20p
Amelia Jane Again  20p

First Term at Malory Towers  20p
Last Term at Malory Towers  20p
Second Form at Malory Towers  20p
Upper Fourth at Malory Towers  20p
In the Fifth at Malory Towers  20p
Third Year at Malory Towers  20p

Mystery of the Disappearing Cat  20p
Mystery of Holly Lane  20p
Mystery of the Secret Room  20p
Mystery of the Invisible Thief  20p
Mystery of the Vanished Prince  20p
Mystery of the Strange Bundle  20p
Mystery of the Spiteful Letters  20p

A Second Book of Naughty Children  20p
The Adventures of
  Mr. Pink-Whistle  20p
Mr. Pink-Whistle Interferes  20p
Mr. Meddle's Muddles  20p
Mr. Meddle's Mischief  20p

## ENID BLYTON (cont.)

Fifteen-Minute Tales  20p
Twenty-Minute Tales  20p
More Twenty-Minute Tales  20p
Eight O'Clock Tales  20p
The Children's Life of Christ  17p
The Red Storybook  20p
The Yellow Storybook  20p
The Blue Storybook  20p
The Green Storybook  20p
Tales from the Bible  17p

## MARY O'HARA

My Friend Flicka – Part 1  20p
My Friend Flicka – Part 2  20p
Thunderhead – Part 2  12p
Thunderhead – Part 3  12p
Green Grass of Wyoming – Part 1  12p
Green Grass of Wyoming – Part 2  12p
Green Grass of Wyoming – Part 3  12p

## CHRISTINE PULLEIN-THOMPSON

The Open Gate  17p
The Empty Field  17p
The First Rosette  17p
The Second Mount  17p
The Pony Dopers  12p
For Want of a Saddle  20p
The Impossible Horse  20p

## MOLLIE CLARKE
(In Colour)

Rabbit and Fox *and* Skillywidden  25p
Mink and the Fire
*and* Aldar the Trickster  25p

## PAT SMYTHE

A Swiss Adventure  20p
A Spanish Adventure  20p

## ANTONIA FRASER

King Arthur and the Knights of the
  Round Table (Illus. by Rebecca
  Fraser)  40p

## LEWIS CARROLL

Alice's Adventures in Wonderland
  (Original illus.)  25p
Alice's Adventures Through the
  Looking-Glass (Original illus.)  25p

## ARTHUR C. CLARKE

Dolphin Island  12p

## NOEL STREATFEILD

The House in Cornwall  17p

... and many, many more. Enquire at your local bookshop.